"Hana Carolina's *The Inescapable March* is a breathtaking tour--de-force that will sweep fans of dark queer fantasy romance off their feet. A novel about eternal love and damnation, it will squeeze the breath out of you like a beautiful and lethal snake. And you will want some more."

— Seb Doubinsky, author of *The City-States Cycle*

"In this time loop fantasy whose puzzle pieces will reward multiple re-readings, Hana Carolina introduces us to a desperate soldier who takes a magical weapon of warfare and repurposes it into a tool of romance and resurrection. Featuring a heart-wrenching love story between two compelling characters whose yearning for one another will keep you turning the pages, *The Inescapable March* asks those who've loved and lost a simple, terrifying question: How many times would you rewind the clock if it meant saving someone you love from certain death?"

— S. M. Hallow, author of *How to Survive This Fairytale*

"*The Inescapable March* left me breathless—a masterfully executed, immersive time loop that blends the horrors of war with the exquisite tension of unresolved romantic longing. Carolina sweeps us up into Arran and Hyacinth's story immediately, through their playful banter, the harsh words spoken in moments of hurt, true feelings deeply hidden—will-they-or-won't-they wound to a delectable breaking point—until the first stunning moment (of many) arrives... the swooping realization that something has shifted. You are not where you thought you were. You are not *when* you thought you were. And it happens again, and again, a sheer delight each time. Let the story carry you, bury yourself in the lush, rich descriptions, become caught up in Arran and Hyacinth's desperation—to connect, to love...to survive. Carolina does all this so easily and so joyfully that one cannot help but pause and marvel at what she has crafted. *The Inescapable March* is an inescapable delight."

— Jennifer Moffatt, author of *Flirty Dancing*

"*The Inescapable March* is a fantasy, erotic, time-bending story that highlights the love two men share for each other as they face war and destruction. Hana Carolina's evocative writing style is rich with world-building detail and intense emotion as she guides her readers through her characters' depths of desire. You are sure to enjoy this dark fantasy horror romance."

— Linda Gould, host of the *Kaidankai Podcast of Ghost & Supernatural Stories*

"Hana Carolina cements that love is a constant choice to continue moving forward, and through her gorgeous prose and time-warped events, has crafted a stellar debut"

— Lor Gislason, author of *The Flesh Of The Sea*

"Hana Carolina's debut *The Inescapable March* is a glass tesseract of a novella, overlapping and dizzying, shot through with desperation and claustrophobia. It's a lush, intricate story about love and its sharp edges. A story layered like the spell at its heart, where time and space are warped by the magic of a man who has finally realised he's lost what he never had the strength to accept. A must for fans of gorgeous prose and queer mythic narratives."

— CL Hellisen, author of *Cast Long Shadows*

"*The Inescapable March* is a dizzy troop through time. Lyrical and bittersweet, tragic and romantic in equal measure—it lingers long after you finish reading"

— Elou Carroll, author of countless short stories and EIC of *Crow & Cross Keys*

The Inescapable March

Hana Carolina

SPACEBOY BOOKS

Denver, Colorado

Published in the United States by:
Spaceboy Books LLC
1627 Vine Street
Denver, CO 80206
www.readspaceboy.com

Cover features Public Domain art by John Everett Millais, William Catto, Mary Vaux Walcott, and William James Webbe

Interior art by Maciej Kubicki

First printed March 2025

ISBN: 978-1-951393-46-5

Dedicated to Jennifer Moffatt

The Prologue

f all their meetings, this was the one Arran remembered best—the bright flash of Hyacinth's smile from the stage, and the applause rolling as thunder through the room. The heavy curtains closed behind him, burgundy fabric swinging, gold thread shimmering in the candlelight. Hyacinth held on to the hand of the sweaty actor next to him—a tall specimen with coal black hair and chiselled features, not unlike Arran's—before diving into a deep curtsy, triumphant, glowing, his flaxen tresses nearly brushing the floor. He laughed—a full, genuine sound breaking through the noise. The comfort, the ritual, the familiarity, as vivid as always. Normal. As if things could never be any different. And Arran soaked this in—the atmosphere, the cheers, the frantic clapping, the precious ringing of that laugh, before the music ground to a halt, and the wood creaked as the crowd moved on in unison.

Many faces turned towards Arran as he walked into the tavern after the performance, soaked in the summer rain, weary from a rushed morning spent on horseback. The cavalcade of whispers melded into an indistinguishable commotion, until he pulled apart the words. They reflected him like a distorted mirror —*have you seen his tattered armour, the shape of his sword, the knife peeking from his boot, the size of him*—on and on. And then there were the stories, the same he heard in every town. Most punters were neither bold nor stupid enough to ask him to leave and seemed very comfortable resenting him from a distance. Soon enough they would lose interest, or decide curiosity was not worth the risk. They'd get busy feasting on the hot stew, which permeated the air with a heavy fragrance of fat and spices. He'd ignore the disdain in the old publican's eyes, order lukewarm ale which sat sour on his tongue, and settle into a chair by the crackling fire, with the view of the celebrating actors. In a busy tavern, their gossip and agitated conversations might have been no louder than a distant murmur to most, yet were clear to him, even from a few tables away.

"Calm down," Hyacinth instructed his rowdy companions, using his stage voice to cut through, "it's not the final night yet. What's come over you?"

"Tell that to yourself, you show-off." The mousy actress, little more than a girl, scoffed at him from the other side of the table, and motioned at his dark-haired friend. "You put Etain to shame, look at his miserable face."

"Fuck off," Etain said, causing a wave of laughter.

"We all got some awkward cheers and a few misplaced claps, let's not get competitive," Hyacinth teased. "And, you know—I'm not one for violence, but I do my best. I stab this handsome man every night—" He prodded Etain with his elbow. "In the most dramatic scene of the third act, no less. Yet the slaughter seems largely uninspired. Falls flat, as it may. Today was different. I went all in, what can I say? The more time we spend together, the easier it is for me to simulate a murderous rage. I wouldn't venture to guess why." He nodded to himself. "Ciara, was I too good?"

The girl giggled. "You're pathetic and wouldn't hurt a fly."

"I knew the line," Etain grumbled. "You threw me off."

"We all know the line," one of the men further back chimed in. "We only heard it a million bloody times."

Ciara stood and puffed her chest with feigned pride. "Why—" She croaked, cleared her throat, and tried again, enunciating each word. "Why might such dread fill my breast, as if death itself lingered only a slither beyond my sight?" Her gaze wandered over the punters crowded around their tables until they found Arran, sitting alone. He stared at Hyacinth with such intensity, she froze, and shivered.

"Not subtle, that," Hyacinth summarised.

"You'd write better?" Etain asked.

Ciara rubbed her shoulders and forced a smile. "Hyacinth's talents know no bounds," she proclaimed, still standing. "He acts, he writes, he sings. He is a revelation, the brightest of lights shining down on us from the firmament up above." She reached towards the ceiling before her eyes gravitated to Arran again. "So bright, he attracts moths and flies."

Hyacinth blinked at her and turned to Etain. "The first time I killed you, I played it as a direct offensive. Then I realised that's the furthest from an imaginative interpretation—obvious, and therefore boring. So I tried to lose control, surprise myself, almost mirror your shock." He flinched. "Not right either."

"No, that much is obvious," Etain said with a mix of bitterness and amusement. "We all know mirroring me can only bring mediocre results."

"Oh, no," Hyacinth protested. "Don't sell yourself short. That time you died—when was it?"

"On Thursday?" Ciara helped.

"Yes, on Thursday." He nodded at her. "It moved me. That last twitch—masterful, truly. Heightened, yet naturalistic. Made me think of—" He appeared lost for a moment, before shaking off the memory. "Regardless, you should try that again. Very effective."

"Sure," Etain said, anger simmering beneath the word.

"But what I was trying to say—" Hyacinth spoke with haste. "Well, the key to my bit was to want to kill you, actually want it. Plan it, do it, just to discover that reality is a far cry from imagined success." He paused, then continued with slow purposefulness. "Wanting and having—those are two very different things. That moment—when the blade sinks into your flesh and there's no return, that's the exact moment I realise that."

Ciara began slow clapping, and Hyacinth rolled his eyes at her. She beamed.

"Anyway—um. I do apologise for getting carried away," Hyacinth said to Etain. "I was so eager to get this right, I didn't consider the difficulties you might face, you know, bleeding out as you do, which seems challenging enough without my interference."

"See?" Ciara raised her voice. "He's not selfish, just self-centred. There's a difference."

"Ciara—" Hyacinth started, then noticed she was hugging herself, as if cold. "You alright?"

"Yeah, I'm—" She let her hands fall. "Have you seen him?" She nodded towards Arran's figure huddled by the entrance. Hidden in the shadows by the open door, with the flickering fire behind him, he was little more than a flat outline, still to an unnatural extent. Ciara strained her eyes, as if hoping that would make him seem more human. "I think—I'm sure it's one of them."

Hyacinth threw a glance in that direction, casual and nonchalant, and stopped dead, failing to hide his surprise. "Um—" He ran a hand through his hair and suppressed a smile. Arran nodded at him, and Hyacinth looked away with a grin, glad Ciara was too preoccupied to notice. Realising she still expected an answer, he tried to recall her words, straining his acting skills to their limit to appear indifferent. "And who are *them*, exactly?"

"You know, the enchanted soldiers."

"Enchanted soldiers?" Hyacinth repeated with profound scepticism.

"You know what I mean. Etain, what did they call them, you remember?"

"Cursed knights?"

"Not all of them were knights." Ciara waved him off. "Magical warriors?"

"Why not, I guess." Etain shrugged.

"Or even better—necromancers," Ciara whispered, far too enthused.

"What?" Hyacinth appeared a tad overwhelmed.

"Well, aren't they supposed to resurrect the dead, or something?" Ciara asked, as if that was a normal question. "Or travel in time?" Seeing their confused expressions, she hesitated. "Or—or attack people in a bout of warrior-rage? Was that what it was?"

"Complete nonsense," Hyacinth snapped, regaining his balance. "Those are myths and legends. Ghost stories to horrify the children, no more, nor less."

She scoffed. "He's no ghost. And he's interested in you. An admirer, perhaps."

Hyacinth chuckled. "I wish." He looked past Ciara and straight at Arran, meeting his eyes for a fleeting moment before turning back to her.

"Mother did tell me about them when I was little, I'll admit as much," she said. "Doesn't mean it's all made up."

"Aren't you little now?" Etain asked.

"Don't be silly." Ciara took a sip of her ale, as if to prove a point. "Weren't most of them executed when —" She struggled to find the right words. "When they were no longer of use? The ones that they managed to catch, that is. Dangerous monsters, mother said. Murderous beasts."

"One would think you're old enough not to repeat what others say without thinking," Hyacinth said, fingers tapping on the table, tone ice-cold. "He can hear you, you know."

Ciara's heart accelerated and she grew paler in the flickering light, but then she laughed it off. "First you say they don't exist, and now you're trying to scare me."

"Maybe you deserve to be scared."

"Hy, stop that," Etain tried without much conviction. He turned towards Arran for the first time, and was taken aback. "Shouldn't we be telling someone?"

"Telling someone what?" Hyacinth asked.

"You're the one who should be scared." Ciara raised her voice at him, ignoring Etain, and pointed at

Arran, not at all shy about attracting his attention. "He's looking at you."

Hyacinth blinked, and appeared disappointed, almost at himself. "He's not a threat."

"Hyacinth, shouldn't we—" Etain started again.

"Right." Hyacinth let out a tired sigh. "That's quite enough."

"What do you mean?" Ciara asked.

"You both stay here." Hyacinth rose from his chair with a blasé attitude of someone who'd done this hundreds of times. "I'll see what he wants."

"Are you fucking stupid?" Ciara hissed, just to be ignored.

Etain didn't say a word, perhaps more willing to trust Hyacinth—or simply more used to him. He watched with profound resignation as Hyacinth manoeuvred between the tables, recognising, better than others in the room, the eagerness in his step.

A few heads turned. But most conversations continued undisturbed. When it became clear where he was heading—and Arran welcomed him with a knowing smirk, not threatening at all—people began to notice, curiosity rippling through the crowd.

Hyacinth didn't seem to mind the eyes on him any more than he did on stage, and stood by Arran's table, as relaxed as one could be, letting the moment last, basking in the attention, whatever the kind. "Greetings, mysterious stranger." Thumbs pushed behind his belt, a snide smile on his lips, he was balancing on the verge of self-parody. "Are you here for me?"

Arran laughed—deep and joyful—surprising himself, and everyone listening, except for Hyacinth, the hostility around them fading into the background. "What makes you think that? I'm after some cold ale on a hot summer night, that's all."

Hyacinth walked up closer, leaned on the table, and grabbed the pitcher from Arran's hand, not hearing the few outraged gasps, which were so clear to Arran, yet aware of them all the same. He took a sip and scrunched his nose in a display of exaggerated disgust. "Cold? You're in the wrong place, then. Maybe we should take it elsewhere."

Arran stared past him, noting the commotion at the actors' table, and frowned. "Etain wasn't too worried when he thought I might tear you to shreds, but he is worried now."

"He should be." Hyacinth feigned a serious tone. "It would be best if he accepted defeat. Comes to him easier on stage. Although, to be fair, it's a difficult thing for a man to realise he can't compete."

Arran raised his brows and took another glance around the room. "Is this smart?" The tension around them intensified by the minute.

"You're the one who chose to make this public."

"I'm not sure about that."

"You wanted me to sneak out into the night? Meet you in the dark woods, maybe?"

"You're becoming too big for your own good. Gossip travels."

"Fuck, I hope. You know what they say—only one thing worse than being talked about."

"Will you be as relaxed when they boo you off the stage tomorrow?"

"Let them try." Hyacinth sounded assertive enough, but Arran could sense his hesitation.

He hummed to himself, not convinced. "Go back to them. Meet me at the stables."

"Really? You'll wait for me like my loyal groom?"

Arran gave him his best what-the-fuck-are-you-talking-about look. "Hyacinth, it might be difficult for you to hear, but you don't have servants, or a husband-to-be. Or even a horse."

"Not for the lack of trying." Hyacinth put the pitcher back on the table, and leaned closer, reaching for a stray hair trapped in the clasp of Arran's leather pauldron.

Arran pulled back.

A few soldiers sitting nearby gave them pointed looks. Etain raised from the table—brave enough for that, but not much else. Ciara began to whisper to an actress sitting next to her, gesticulating with such frantic urgency she knocked over her pint. The glass rolled across the floor.

The wooden panels creaked under the weight of moving feet. The conversations grew louder.

"Out," Arran whispered to Hyacinth, the venom

in his voice unsettling them both.

The humid air outside hit them with sharp, chilly freshness—wind carried from across the rain-soaked wheat fields, the light fragrance of lilacs. They both paused, somehow astounded by the stillness of the night, forgotten amidst the commotion of the hot, crowded rooms they left behind.

Candles glimmered behind the glazed windows, glass panels glowing stains of ochre against the muted, bluish darkness surrounding them. The inn's entrance was nestled amongst multi-coloured wildflowers. White and purple alyssum in heavy pots hanging from the roofed frame above their heads was still dripping, although the sky was clear and speckled with stars.

The outside tables stood empty, in haunted silence, the uproar of the tavern muffled by the door. The church on the other side of a cobbled road was engulfed in shadows, grey walls blinking from behind the swinging branches of a weeping willow. Graves, the moss-green crosses and crumbling skulls, peeked at them from behind a low, stone fence.

Arran motioned for Hyacinth to follow him, and he did, passing through a narrow road behind the brewery, until they were sheltered underneath a broad crown of an oak tree, separated from them by a garden wall—a dead end, lit by nothing but the moon, out of earshot.

Hyacinth was not nearly as cocky as before. His

racing heart thumped in Arran's temples, his transformation from a cad to a spooked rabbit almost complete.

"Never—" Arran started through gritted teeth—as calm as he could force himself to be. "Never do that again."

Hyacinth stood there in silence, hyperventilating, unwilling to face him, and stared at a single ivy stem sneaking in where the mortar crumbled away. He picked off one of the leaves and let it fall to the ground. "I hate it when they treat you like a leper."

"And this is supposed to help?"

"It's not what—" He took a deep breath. "You know I didn't mean to cause any trouble."

"Was this in any way hard to predict?"

"Well, you were happy to play along," Hyacinth snapped, and regretted it in an instant.

"That's true. Maybe the next time I see you, I should pretend not to know you."

Hyacinth was stunned for a second, genuine hurt making his eyes take on a glassy glow.

Something twisted in Arran's gut, and he wanted to stop what he had started, but wasn't sure how. Layers upon layers of frustration within him were squeezed together so tight, he could no longer tell them apart. The only thing he knew was that Hyacinth was at the centre of it somehow, and that Hyacinth knew it too.

"I'm sorry. I'm sorry, alright?" Hyacinth sounded

upset, and Arran didn't like it one bit. "I'm sorry about Ciara, too."

"She's not your responsibility. Nor is she the problem." Arran lowered his voice to a whisper. "It bothers you when I get the wrong type of attention but dragging me into a cheap pantomime—Great fucking idea, indeed."

"Maybe it was. Maybe this—" He gestured between them, quarrelling in the middle of an empty road. "Maybe that's still better than—"

"Better than what?"

Hyacinth shook his head. "What brings you here, really?"

"Nothing much."

"Did you see the play?"

"Why would I? I've sat through enough of your theatrics."

"I guess that's right." Hyacinth seemed defeated by the admission, losing his impetus. "But—um. I was beginning to worry. It's been a while."

Arran hummed in agreement.

"Too long," Hyacinth tried.

"We don't have a schedule."

"Arran, please."

"Weren't you supposed to leave tomorrow?"

"The day after."

"Are you leaving, or staying?"

"Why would I stay?"

"Etain is local, isn't he?"

Hyacinth let out a bitter laugh. "Of course."

"It's a simple question."

"You always get so touchy when it's a man, have you noticed? You sit around, unconcerned, yet listen in with such great attention."

"Not without reason."

"I bet." Hyacinth folded his arms across his chest.

Arran narrowed his eyes and controlled his voice. "Men get aggressive when you act like it was nothing and leave."

"But it was nothing. And this is a city, not a middle-of-nowhere village like when—" He looked away, trying to calm down, realising he might be undermining his own argument.

"Hy—"

"I'm alright." He shrugged, trying to hide the tension in his shoulders.

"Hyacinth, all I'm saying—he's got the self-conceit and the muscle."

"He's a kind man, you don't know him."

"Fine, then don't rub it in his face." Arran's voice softened. "You're better than this."

"It's worth the risk for me, I suppose." The words came out harsher than he'd meant—one step away from calling Arran a coward.

"We're not doing that."

"Sure, you're right." Hyacinth was not agreeing at all, clinging to anger, as if that was easier. "What would you rather do instead? What's the point of all this?"

"There's a war brewing, as I'm sure you've heard."

"Yes, um—" Thrown off in an instant, he was not eager to discuss the news. "I—I thought nothing was certain. But people do talk." His eyes grew larger for a blink. "Fuck, do they ever."

"Yeah, then start listening."

"But—"

"I'm serious." Arran stared him down, responding to Hyacinth's pointless hesitation with greater concern than he was prepared for. "Don't be caught with your pants down, for fuck's sake. Think before choosing jobs, be careful when you travel. Start saving—no matter how challenging that might be—and decide where you can go when—"

"Don't you want to go with me?"

"It's not happening yet." Arran sounded colder than intended.

"I meant now."

"I don't think so."

Hyacinth blinked at him, somehow more concerned about this than the war. "Arran, what's wrong? Was I really that unbearable today?"

"I'm only passing through."

"Then where are you headed?"

"Does it matter?"

"Really?" Hyacinth failed to suppress a wet chuckle. "These days you're always 'passing through' when you come to see me." He shook his head. "I haven't changed, it's you. You know that, right?" He waited, not expecting an answer. "I understand the limits. And I'm fine, see? It was all in good jest, nothing more. It's always been perfectly fucking obvious you wouldn't—" Blood rushed to his cheeks, and he hesitated. "Your, um, let's call it 'lack of interest' was exactly what I was playing with. That's— that was the joke."

"You're pushing this too far."

"I miss you." Hy put his whole heart into the words.

Arran's skin began to crawl. "I should go."

"Arran, please. I understand, I swear. Let's go back to the way we were."

"I'll see you around." Arran gave him a nod, a tight smile, and began walking away.

"I don't know what else to do. Arran—" Hy launched forward and grabbed his forearm. "Please," he tried again. "Please, tell me what to do."

The request was genuine, and the pleading went on longer than Arran wished to recall. He has never seen Hy so helpless. But he left all the same.

Arran wasn't sure why he remembered this meeting with such devastating clarity. He wasn't one to dwell on the past, not one to think of a conversation over and over, not one to care about the details, unless they mattered. And yet, here it was— fresh in his mind, returning, every painful minute as vivid and distinct as if he was living through it again, nagging at him.

The last time I saw him alive, he thought, and flinched, his mind slipping into some form of insanity. Because it was not true. Absolute nonsense.

In fact, Arran knew he'd seek Hyacinth out as soon as the war broke out, which was exactly what he did. No choice but to—to travel with him as they did, to make sure he was safe. Their stupid quarrels amounted to nothing. They would meet again, go through the same motions. The only thing worse than repeating the circle would be breaking it. And Arran could be quick to anger but was not thoughtless. He wouldn't let this pettiness put Hyacinth at risk.

Yet, he'd find himself thinking about that day the same way he thought about the final time he saw his mother—the faint smile on her pale face, hollow cheeks, hands holding on to the arms of her favourite chair as if it could help her. He'd go through it again— the evening he had left his hometown, the last glance he took at the stone buildings bathed in orange light before they disappeared behind the bend. The first time he killed a man—the stillness of his widened pupils, the last breath like a relieved sigh.

All those memories had nothing to do with leaving Hyacinth that day. Nothing at all. They couldn't have. That much he knew for sure.

Chapter 1
The Art of Letting Things Die

A robin said: The Spring will never come,
And I shall never care to build again.
A Rosebush said: These frosts are wearisome
My sap will never stir for sun or rain.
The half Moon said: These nights are fogged and slow,
I neither care to wax nor care to wane.
The Ocean said: I thirst from long ago,
Because earth's rivers cannot fill the main.
When springtime came, red Robin built a nest,
And trilled a lover's song in sheer delight.
Gray hoarfrost vanished, and the Rose with might
Clothed her in leaves and buds of crimson core.
The dim Moon brightened. Ocean sunned his crest,
Dimpled his blue, - yet thirsted evermore.

~ Christina Georgina Rossetti

uring his training, Arran had cast a few spells on himself he shouldn't have. They hit him harder than tiredness, alcohol, a fever, even

the pain of a deep wound, all that sharp blades could do to his bones and skin. His mind would scatter, breaking reality into a million pieces that didn't fit, forcing him to create a makeshift mosaic out of the familiar shards of his thoughts and feelings. There were monsters there, and a lurking realisation that "familiar" wasn't quite the word, no. At the crunch point, it was clear that Arran knew nothing of himself, and liked it that way, too. But he did learn how to navigate those moments when his memory would fail him, logic crumbled, emotions seized control, and the world appeared unreal—a blend of random colours, shapes, and impressions—unreachable, and artificial, a pathetic copy, like those paintings Hyacinth dragged him all the way to the capital to see. Perhaps Hyacinth would have coped better than Arran. After all, he preferred representations to reality, yearned for the impossible, and saw connections even when there weren't any. But Arran did handle it, even back then. And he'd improved since.

There was a pride in endurance and a relief in denial, the two vices he stuck with—whether through necessity, or choice, he wasn't sure. Oh, he could foresee the course of a war, tell the panicky nonsense spread by ignorant attention-seekers apart from valid information passed on by those with all the access, and no ability to shut the fuck up. He could choose the right paths, traverse broken villages and towns, face death lurking around every corner, find sustenance when others starved, kill to survive, step over corpses and ignore the smell of decay—that was what he was made for, after all. The more the others wailed and gave into despair, the calmer he became, drifting through the cool waters of his indifference, refreshed and impermeable. What a comfort that was, what a skill in the world such as theirs. Or maybe his impassivity was what Hyacinth called it, "posturing" and "bullshit". To some extent, perhaps.

Hyacinth was so eager to point out Arran's "frustrating" tendency to stretch himself further than any person should. But he wasn't really "a person" was he? And that was great luck for Hyacinth who was, himself, quite a stretch for Arran, in fact. Always, more so now.

Arran was no longer a warrior, but he was accustomed to tragedies to an extent that reached far beyond the vast bounds of Hyacinth's artistic imagination. Only something was different when this slaughter began. He could tell by the distant inkling of despair building in his gut, the echoes of his youth, all the times he toyed with magic and found himself biting much, much more than he could chew.

The long wait ended with a surprise attack on a town Arran couldn't name—a shock to all those used to the never-ending anticipation, the "almost", which lasted years, and gave them something akin to a sense of safety. Arran should have known, should have been more prepared, but was caught unawares, no different than an average punter, no less uneasy, and for reasons he couldn't explain.

The first thing he did was ask around for Hyacinth, he was sure. But he didn't remember what he had heard, or who told him where to look. He wouldn't admit this to Hyacinth, but he didn't remember how he found him either, or where they met, nor what they said. He didn't know what day it was, only that the winter was about to end.

No matter. He could deduct what he didn't know, as surely as he could recognise the season from the grainy sprinkle of green appearing in the warmest stretches of lands he travelled through, tell time by how fast the blotches of warmth were replaced by the chilling breath of the evening when the last rays of sunshine disappeared from his face. The dropping temperature made him shiver, thin fabric stuck to his back, sweaty from exertion.

Where was he rushing?

He shifted his weight, and his horse slowed down from a gallop to a walk with a quiet snort.

The town was miles behind him. The humid forest air smelled of pine, and his chest was tense, so tense no deep breath could offer him relief. A persistent memory, which offered him answers he didn't want to hear, kept breaking through as surely as the hazy, pastel colours of the sunset glimmered between the rain clouds darkening the sky.

The gossip of the army moving south turned out

to be true. A trail of burned ground served as an undeniable proof to those who preferred to distrust the discordant voices. The connecting tracks were filling up with hunched figures and packed wagons, wheels unsettling the sandy roads. The light buzzing of unease was borderline audible in every settlement Arran and Hyacinth travelled through. War had followed them, a march as steady as the passage of time.

And yet, not long after sunrise, Hyacinth had turned away, his back visible for a while amongst a colourful mix of strangers in a busy market. Arran hadn't called after him when he could have. The lump in his throat was still there, somehow, all these hours later.

He remembered wanting to avoid pointless staring, so his eyes lingered on a young girl selling flowers, a fresh-grass-green dress, and a light smile. She was rearranging a small bouquet, binding thin stems together with determination bordering on cruelty. Her hair slipped onto her face, but she didn't mind, lost in the task. Her eyes, starved after winter, devoured the yellow of the daffodils, the deep hue of the bluebells, the thick, plump leaves crunching under her fingers.

And when he had looked ahead again, there wasn't a trace of Hyacinth anymore.

Good riddance, he had thought, walking off.

There were still a couple of things to attend to.

The town was so small, it was hardly surprising he had found himself passing by the tavern they stayed at the night before. It was a sturdy building snuggled against the castle wall, hidden within a small enclosure, the door propped open, guests pouring in and out. The White Horse Inn, he read, as if he didn't already know. The sign was worn down, the rearing animal crumbling, wood peeking from behind the paint. The shapes behind the horse deteriorated so much, he could no longer discern them, but there was red and orange, almost like fire.

Arran never crossed the threshold, just noted the proximity to the gate, the narrow street leading towards it, and the two stone lions at either side that stared back at him with hollow eyes. One's head was tilted as if it was curious, its front paw frozen mid-step.

Some hunched figures pushed past him—offended looks, as if he was blocking the entrance. He was nowhere near. City guards, barely half a dozen. One had a deep scar, running from his cheek bone to his jaw, still inflamed. Another had a limp, so small, most people would miss it. Perhaps it wasn't offence, just distrust. Maybe they could sense the humming of magic under his skin, recognise the animal-like smoothness of his movements, the darkness behind his eyes. When a few of them turned back, Arran squeezed the handle of his sword—less a threat than a gentle warning. Neither side wanted the trouble. He nodded at them in silent acknowledgment, and they nodded back, moving on.

The house he was summoned to was at the edge of town—stone walls crumbling, the roof sloping to the side. The woman, who opened the creaking door dressed in a long robe with edges caked in mud, looked away when letting him in. Some believed it was bad luck to stare into his eyes and were eager to protect themselves. It was as if they expected fate to spare them, still, despite already dealing with misfortune terrible enough to require his assistance.

"He went with the others," she said as soon as they sat by a wobbly table in her cramped kitchen, a black cat slipping by Arran's ankle. "He went with them and never came back."

"What do you wish had happened?" A jug with a chipped edge, full of souring milk, stood by Arran's hand. The sickly-sweet smell permeated the room, strong enough to make him nauseous.

"I don't care what he does. As long as he stays." She spoke with the unwavering confidence of a person who didn't understand the implications of her own words.

Arran nodded, something between resignation and an understanding.

"It's just like a dream, isn't it?" She shifted in the chair and scratched her arm, staring into the floor. There was something childish about her, an awkward jerkiness in her fingers, but the skin around her eyes was dry and weathered—whether tiredness or age, he couldn't tell. "Just a bad dream, yes?" She looked at him, no hesitation this time.

"No." Arran leaned into the back of the wooden chair, splats biting into his spine. "It feels real. You won't be able to tell the difference."

"But you'll guide me through this?"

"No, you'll be under the spell. I'm just how you get there."

"And what about him? Will I actually meet him? Is he—" She reconsidered her questions, nervous to ask about what she was most eager to find out. "Will he know I tried this?"

"It really is him. But he won't know or remember. He'll only live through the final outcome you choose."

"That I choose?" The control this implied struck a note.

"Yes, the spell will take you outside of space and time. It's a maze and everything becomes more and more muddled the longer you stay. But if you manage that, you'll be everywhere and nowhere at once and you'll reach for the moment you want, any moment, and do what you want, pull any thread, try again if necessary."

"Try again? Can I?" Something sneaked into her voice—hope, perhaps. "How many times?"

"As many as you need."

She blinked, no longer confused. "Then why are you here?"

"What?"

"Can't you fix this for yourself?" There was a hint of malice in her smirk. "Aren't you a powerful mage? And a fighter, isn't that true? That you can make yourself stronger than any man by whispering a few, silly words?"

"That's beside the point."

"Or is that what you want? To be a cheap seller of second chances?"

"It's better than being paid to torture or kill." There was no anger in his voice, no threat, yet her eyes widened, pupils blown.

He shook his head and whispered the spell under his breath.

The milk in the jug was no longer coagulated, or thick—a smooth white surface, a snow on a December morning before anyone left home. And she straightened out her back, dress somehow neater, face fresher, a glimmer of something he couldn't quite place in her look.

She stood up and faced her husband, a tall man with broad shoulders, and their conversation melted into a cavalcade of sounds—familiar patterns, yet indistinguishable, like a song of a language Arran didn't speak. They filled the kitchen with many afternoons, mornings, and nights, inhabiting every corner, moving in a continuous dance of their daily lives, the air thick with the smell of hundreds of meals. As the clatter of cutlery grew louder and more persistent, so did the voices—yelling mixed with laughter, whispers, a cry of a child, doors opening and closing.

Finally, she stopped and stood in the middle of the room staring at a figure in front of her—a woman, the same as her, herself, and they both froze. The husband left, as he always did, the door slamming behind him. One of her followed him and the other stepped away, escaping the dizzying rhythm, and sat in front of Arran, alone again, a hand twitching.

"That's fine, I'm done." Her voice swelled with tears. "You can go."

"You sure?"

"Yes." She nodded, appearing not as certain as she was determined, using a corner of her sleeve to wipe her eyes.

He thought about her, as she was in that moment, when riding away, the forest quiet around him—that everyday bravery giving up required sometimes. The strength he somehow lacked.

"Fine," he said then, already rising from the chair, eager to leave her house, the hateful, suffocating space overcrowded with unwanted memories.

"There's been no point since our son—" She paused for a sharp intake of breath. When she spoke, her tone was controlled again. "Can you cast the spell on someone who's dead?"

Arran sat back down, a weird feeling nagging at

him. "I can," he said, his throat dry to the point of being scratchy. "Anyone who existed, even for a blink, had their moment. I can grab onto that, so yes, I can."

"Just like that?"

"I'd need a body, or whatever remains of it." Arran was somehow embarrassed to admit that—a gruesome detail, irrelevant to this conversation. An image of open eyes—unmoving, blue, fading to white, flashed through his mind, and his pulse picked up. "But I wouldn't."

"Why not?"

"The dead can't do it alone. I'd have to cast a spell on myself too, and that gets—" He considered many possibilities, some more gruesome than others, before settling on "—complicated." He punctuated the word with a tight smile. "Many have tried. Most cannot change a thing. And being trapped in endless repetition, with death as the only certain outcome— that's hell. I wouldn't do that to someone, or myself."

"Hell? That's what you think hell is?" She let out a wet chuckle. "That's just life."

Arran found it hard to leave the town. He had walked through the market again, sunshine sharp and blinding, intercutting streams of people around him, a frenzy of colours, life humming with unwavering insistence, tones hushed but for the sellers—baritones sounding above the sea of moving heads. He circled the stalls as the merchants were beginning to wrap up. After a warm day, the smell of fish and decaying meat was harsh and oppressive. A mass of bodies was passing him by. *Too many*, he had thought.

For what? his mind snapped back, then emptied.

Those moments became hours. And another few, until the afternoon slipped into evening, and the choice was between racing to the next town over or having to stay.

And staying would have obviously been a terrible idea. *For fuck's sake.*

He shifted his weight, leaning into the saddle, and his horse stopped, hooves digging into the soft ground. "Hush, Beira, hush," he said to her, although she didn't make a sound.

The forest was quiet too, something ghostly about the evening song of the young birds, the breeze sneaking in between the bare branches, fresh buds barely there. It was like icy water running through his hair, and down his back, the wind.

Hyacinth always hated that, being caught on the road at sundown in March. He'd call it "the wretched vestiges of winter," his shoulders trembling, breath visible, and tone offended, as if the weather hurt him on purpose. He'd be wearing something ridiculous, of course—layers upon layers of silk he couldn't really afford, a hat which was purely ornamental. Wool was too common for him, but so was the cold he despised, even more so once a sunny day settled the heat in his bones. *Yes, sunshine would promise him mellow nights, the shuffle of leaves, cherry trees in full bloom, and fool him* easily, because he was eager to be fooled. *No, it was not spring yet.*

And Hyacinth was no stranger to disappointment.

Was he?

Arran's heartbeat picked up the pace. Fuck this unruly mind of his.

Just a few weeks back, they rode past a scorched corpse of a town. The soldiers pushed the inhabitants against their own defensive walls—panicked, trapped behind the gate they themselves bolted and secured, crushed in a futile attempt to escape. Even Arran was grateful the bodies looked somehow abstract when covered in frozen mud, shrouded in a thick layer of ice, most shapes dissolved to the point of incoherency. Hyacinth bent over and threw up, the most florid comment a poet could make.

He must be in the tavern now, Arran thought. *There would be a fireplace radiating pleasant heat, eyes already set on some interested party who would drag him up the stairs and make him forget wars, and false springs.*

It would be the right kind of person too. Someone who'd listen to the stories about his adventures, nod when he explains his writing ambitions, and agree his singing is, in fact, as good as his acting. Someone who'd actually want him. And that was better—simple, enough to make him happy.

No, that was a lie. It had been a long time since Hyacinth was either happy, or safe. Too long, that much was clear.

The night before, Hyacinth had been great on stage, as always—every gesture brimming with emotion, a marvel amongst the stiff locals. But once he entered the tavern ready to celebrate, something shifted. His smiles shone all the same, but never reached his eyes, shoulders tense, hair damp and stuck to his forehead. He moved through the crowd with caution, as if it was a wild, unsettled beast, ready to swallow him up.

"Sing," the few who followed him from the theatre demanded, "sing."

So he did, his voice hoarse and strained. An actor who made a jittery singer without a spark was a surprise to no one but his only friend in the audience.

In the middle of his set, a blackbird fell through the window—a dark smudge hitting the ground by his foot, its beak opening and closing with no sound, one wing limp, the other stretching out and twitching one last time before it stilled. Hyacinth stared, stunned, mouth moving wordlessly, then looked straight at Arran as if asking for something.

Hyacinth's heart started to race, thumping like a pulse in Arran's own temples, his smell turned acidic, look changed—an involuntary twitch, skin turning ashen white, lips bloodless. He blinked. The colours returned to his face as quickly as they had disappeared, and he shook his head, chest heaving, startled by his own response.

Arran took a step towards him, then stopped,

eyes questioning.

When Hyacinth took the bird in his hands, and walked to put it on the windowsill, floorboards creaking under his feet, the crowd followed his every step—some with fear, some with uneasy laughter. Others recoiled with a gasp, as if he was diseased, a cavalcade of whispers rising around him. Hyacinth didn't have to hear the words to know what they said. A few left. Those who stayed met him with vacant stares.

And yet, he finished his performance. Only it took a long while for his voice to stop shaking. His eyes kept drifting to Arran who heard every quiver, every delay, every mistake in the songs they both knew by heart—songs he'd heard Hyacinth perform hundreds of times with unwavering confidence. It hurt. And it didn't get better even when Hyacinth seemingly did. There was a meaning to this, and it was escaping them.

The audience was not as perceptive. The mood changed, voices kept joining in until the atmosphere turned rowdy, and soon everything appeared fine, more than fine—coins bouncing off the tables, rounds being ordered, the whole crowd swinging. Arran was the only island amongst the crushing waves of human flesh—hands waving, feet stomping and stumbling, beer splashing. The smell of stew, stale ale, and old sweat was overwhelming.

A normal night.

By the end, Hyacinth's voice dropped, his breath a cloud of hot, alcohol-infused air, face covered in a sheer layer of sweat, collar yellowing on the edges. His hands turned grabby, so fucking needy, demanding, the pressure unbearable, pushing Arran—already tired and worried enough—to the breaking point with such self-assurance, one would be forgiven for thinking that was the plan all along.

Shaking off Hyacinth's hands was a bizarre kind of crime, so different from piercing a sword through a soldier. Should be trivial yet felt so much worse because it was not blessed with a sense of duty, or granted the sweet oblivion of impersonality. It felt like hitting a child.

"We might be dead tomorrow," Hyacinth said, once all his other arguments failed.

Sure, Arran thought, *we might.* Hyacinth could have—should have—used that line on the boisterous redhead who clapped with above-average enthusiasm, or the shy daughter of the tavern owner who was desperate to be convinced, but there it was, ringing in Arran's ears like a bitter insult, spoken with undeniable, heart-wrenching sincerity.

Something about that image stuck with him, an unshakable vividness of Hyacinth's lips pressed together in a resigned, sad smile, the silence filling their dingy room once he finally ran out of words, his shirt unbuttoned and hanging off his shoulder. He looked...lost.

Arran blinked a few times, and emerged from the memory, grasping the only point that mattered. *It was a mistake*, he thought, *a selfish and stupid mistake to leave him behind.*

The forest around him was sharp again, each biting gasp of wind more stinging than the previous. There must have been an owl nearby, a low hoot resonating in between bare trees, hollow and haunting.

The superstitious townsfolk, the people who saw their future in scattered rat bones and trusted the stars to tell them what to do—those who stepped back when a blackbird fell through a window and who would kill a black cat for crossing their way—they'd say hearing an owl meant someone you love was about to die.

His mother had mocked that once, back when they could still walk together. "There's not enough loved ones in the world to cover the hoots," she'd said. "There's a logic to seeing it as a bad omen, though. If you're silly enough to think it means something, you shouldn't be trusted with the road at night. And when things are unsettling enough that an owl can spook you, you'd best trust your gut before things turn sordid."

"It's because relatives stay up long past dusk to sit by the sickbed and hear the owls through the window," he'd explained back then, although he liked her interpretation better.

"Well, in that case, we have much to look forward to," she sneered.

Arran couldn't sleep the night before. The tavern was bustling—steps, whispered conversations, sighs and distant moans. A mockingbird sang against a backdrop of other birds' aggressive chirping—a discordant chorus intercut with the even, deep breaths beside him. Hyacinth was facing away, the space between them wider than necessary, his bright hair scattered on the pillow. His chest rose and fell in a calming rhythm, but Arran was full of unease.

Hyacinth let out a soft gasp, and his breath became unsteady. A twitch unsettled the bed. "What did you say?"

"I didn't say anything."

"Weird. I could swear I heard you above all the noise." He sounded breathless and moved, yet remained completely still, an outline against the window. "I thought you'd leave me behind. I really did. Thank god you're here."

Arran froze, then stared into the back of Hyacinth's head. "You're making no sense. Just sleep," he snapped, but to his own surprise his voice broke.

"But I don't want to," Hyacinth mumbled, drifting away. "I don't want to—Arran?"

He hummed in response.

"Tell me we'll be fine."

"We'll be fine," he repeated without thought.

Hyacinth stirred, and his breath grew even again,

birds audible once more.

Beira kept pawing the ground, as if asking why they remained still in the middle of an empty road as the last remaining rays of light were fading. She shook, skin rippling.

"Easy," he whispered, one hand patting her neck, the other holding up the reins. "We're going back."

The decision brought him more relief than he wished to admit. In his mind Hyacinth was there, in that room, still, the same as he left him, waiting to be found.

Before he turned Beira around, a glimmer of movement attracted his attention, a dark shape emerging from the fog.

He wondered who would travel at this time through a deserted road such as this. But it was nothing, no reason to stop and stare. And yet his eyes stayed fixed, trying to pierce the mist, drawn to the figure as the distance between them shrank bit by bit. A blurry outline— the trees behind it sharp black lines scribbled across an ink blue sky, the scene drenched in pallid white.

Something familiar about the light sway of the body on the horse. Arran tilted his head in concentration, and the silhouette mirrored his movement. A thin contour of a neck and shoulders sharpened, then became hazy again. Arran's pulse quickened—why, he wasn't sure. It was just a rider at a distance, his horse speeding up.

An intense pang of fear hit him hard—a piercing, icy bite in his chest, Beira freezing underneath. He wanted to say something but couldn't. The black hair, the broad figure clad in tattered armour, the brown, swift horse—stains of colour grew distinct, until the obvious was impossible to deny. When he understood, Beira stomped, nose flaring.

Similar, so similar, he thought, but his body already knew the truth his mind was afraid to admit. He was looking into his own, dark eyes, at the shape of his own body, a carbon copy of Beira. His own face was indifferent and focused, staring with no awareness, riding straight ahead, calmly returning to the town.

"I've been wondering," Hyacinth said years ago, "when you tear through time, can that leave a trace?"

"A trace?"

"Yes, something others can see. There are ghost stories like what you describe. These stories people bring from battlefields, you know, the ones where their friend would come back pale and terrified, swear he saw himself walking towards what turned out to be a merciless slaughter—a premonition of certain death."

"These are just stories."

"But everybody has heard at least one, right?" He glanced up from a piece of parchment, ink spilling with the movement.

"Yes, they're common." Arran shrugged. "And

simple—you see yourself, you die."

"But if that's only one possibility, there is still a chance. It's not unavoidable. Why would none of them escape when they still could?" Hyacinth looked at Arran with genuine curiosity, eyes piercing through him.

Arran took a deep breath. His doppelganger smiled, a knowing expression which was alien somehow, and he steered his horse towards the other side of the road. They bypassed Arran, their feet nearly brushing. Arran's heartbeat doubled, then faded as the space between them grew again.

He heard himself swallow, then another distant hoot of an owl, the branches cracking. It was completely dark but for the moon peeking from behind the trees. His eyes watered in the frosty wind. He hesitated, then shook his head with repressed anger, and shifted his hips to turn Beira around, following his shadow, picking up the pace.

There was something weird about Hyacinth—his sloppy singing, the unusual urgency in his tone, that fucking neediness laid bare, and made obvious, after years and years in hiding, after hundreds of innuendos, jokes and suggestive pauses, here it was.

"What do you want?" Hyacinth had snapped, shaking like his life depended on the answer, one of the last things he said before he left, the crowd swarming behind him.

Why now? What Hyacinth wanted was clear from

the start, but he had never been stupid enough to cross that line.

"Quite fancy. Is it your real name?" Arran had asked him the day they met, a century ago.

"I decided it is." Hyacinth shrugged, as if he just made up his own name for Arran's benefit. It was a loud tavern, right after one of his performances. His voice was a little raspy. "Friends call me Hy."

"Your friends?"

He misunderstood and thought Arran didn't hear. "—call me Hy."

Arran crossed his arms, leaning back in the chair. "That's good to know, Hyacinth."

In response, Hyacinth presented him with the widest, most cheeky smile he'd ever seen.

Arran's lips twitched, but he kept his expression stern.

"Well," Hyacinth said after a pause, "if you don't want to be friends, there are alternatives."

Arran suppressed a laugh. "Don't you know who I am?"

"I don't. We've just met."

"Not what I meant," Arran said, now serious.

"I know." Hy matched Arran's seriousness. "But I meant what I said."

And Arran marvelled at that. Back then. Still.

Arran tapped Beira's sides, making her speed up to a gallop, leg firmly hooked behind the girth, rushing her as much as he could, worried they might be too late. If he knew what was at stake, he wouldn't have left. Or, perhaps, he left because he knew. But he shouldn't have. He shouldn't have. He shouldn't have.

The road was long, the town further than he remembered, and time slipped by, sky changing, until every sight appeared unfamiliar, the landscape flattened by the night.

As he got closer, he heard hooves thudding against the ground, the rhythm frantic. A white horse emerged from behind the trees—a blinking presence on a winding road, a bright blotch haloed by blazing, air-bending glow. The smell of smoke hit him, a vivid taster of the tragedy the animal dragged from miles away.

There was no rider. Just a burning wagon, blackened wood crumbling amid flying sparks. The horse's mouth hung open, head swaying, eyes in a frenzy, foam running down its muzzle, the tail already catching the flame.

It let out a loud, roaring neigh as it passed.

Arran barely managed to get Beira out of the way before the wagon swung and crashed into a nearby tree. A broken wheel rolled into leafless bushes.

He left it all behind, urging Beira to go even faster, the trees a blur, until the town emerged—a vast landscape of destruction stretching in front of him, houses like burning caskets, black figures prowling amongst the scattered townspeople. Their blades flashed silver, rising and falling with a berserk glimmer. The deadly glow of the fire fought the heavy, descending darkness, sounds carrying from afar, overwhelming and wild.

It was worse than he expected—so much worse.

The whole day flashed before of his eyes, the worn-down look of the few guards he left behind, the bolted gate and the tavern right beside it. And the people, too many to push past, the heavy market wagons standing in the middle of poky, cobbled roads. He imagined them falling into each other, pressed together with bone-crushing force, blood mixing with mud, hands sliding on the slimy moss-covered stones. And then all he saw was Hyacinth, his stage persona evaporating in an instant, the blackbird at his feet, lips trembling.

It started to rain. The air was thick with fog, the smell earthy. The big, heavy drops turned into hail. The sky above was trapped behind an impenetrable layer of clouds, moving across at a frantic pace, swallowing the moon.

Arran raced ahead, the wind deafening, the bite of the ice sharper as he rode. It was just a short burst, transforming into rain again, but lighter, a relief from the all-encompassing fire, which didn't stay subdued for long.

The first soldier fell back in panicked haste at the sight of the charging rider, and tripped over a body behind him, tumbling down, a spear sliding from his fingers and falling out of his reach.

Arran jumped off Beira, landing on the wet ground with a splash, a towering presence, already reaching for his sword.

The man looked around as if expecting help, hands slipping when he tried to crawl back. When his elbows gave out, he flailed like an overturned beetle, then grasped for the knife in his belt.

All he could see were feet running beside his head, and a frozen mask of a face—cheek squashed into mud, eyes closed, skull cracked open, grey brain crumbling through the fracture. Pinkish bone stood out sharp against the dark crust of blood-matted hair. Smoke stung his eyes, and he kept blinking wildly, but the image remained blurred.

He didn't really look like someone who would slaughter the townspeople around him. There was something childish about the way he kept scrambling backward, although it was obvious he was just buying seconds.

Arran cut through his neck, and in a single swing also brought the sword into the abdomen of a soldier charging at him from behind.

The boy let out a gurgling sound, and bucked, eyes widening, muscles twitching. It was ridiculous how young he was—a teen, nothing more—his skin shiny from sweat and rain.

Arran tasted blood. He must have bitten the inside of his mouth at the sight of the young man clutching onto the blade lodged in him, eyes focused on the point of impact with surprise and disbelief. His irises were sky blue, bright, their shine draining slowly, pupils deep and black, wild from fear. He gasped for air in shocked desperation.

Arran hesitated, not something he could afford. So he stepped forward, driving the sword deeper, slicing through layers of skin like butter, until the blade bumped against the sternum, all nerves alive and wailing.

The boy pressed his lips together in pained determination. Tears flooded his face as he leaned forwards, rib cage refusing to give way. He choked and coughed.

Blood sprayed, warm against Arran's face.

A trembling hand reached for Arran's shoulder in a silent plea. He was healthy, strong. It was taking too long. Neither could look away until a running woman, her dress on fire, ran past with a piercing scream.

Their heads turned, a beat before Arran pushed him off the sword.

The boy's bubbling shriek broke through the noise, body tipping backwards and tumbling to the ground, flesh contorted with spasms.

Arran found it hard to remember why he was there. The houses with straw roofs roared like bonfires, flames reaching high into the sky, burning arrows drawing shining lines above him.

A howl sounded in the distance—animal or human, he couldn't tell.

No one else dared to approach him. Yet.

Beira raised her head, one of her ears twitching and turning towards him.

They were at the edge of town, and he could not drag her into the narrow, labyrinthine streets. But regardless of how often he did it in the past, chasing her away was a challenge this time, and when he grabbed the reins, his hand trembled.

"Stay out of trouble," he whispered, patting her neck.

I'm not coming back. He winced at the thought, so obvious, a chilling echo of the feeling he had when the dark eyes of his doppelgänger returned his look.

What was even the point?

Every dead body scattered on these streets could be Hyacinth's, every unrecognisable, scorched corpse locked in a burning house. He arrived too late. He might scream Hy's name all he wanted, and no one would respond. Perhaps he was truly alone. Perhaps it was his own damn fault. Perhaps they deserved it. Perhaps he'd rather not find him at all, than see him broken and lifeless. Perhaps.

He hummed quietly to himself, still petting Beira.

But then there was Hyacinth waking up to the havoc in the tavern, running down the stairs in blind panic, falling into a mass of bodies behind the door, listening to the battering ram hammering the gate, hoping as he would.

Naive to the last fucking breath, because there

was no escaping where he was.

Arran imagined those unbearable, pleading eyes, and nodded to himself. *Fine. Fucking fine*, he thought. Of course, he'd relent. He still regretted all the times he hadn't.

He whispered some meaningless, tender words at Beira. And, once he ran out of excuses to delay any longer, he removed the reins from her bit, and shooed her away.

She turned towards him one last time, then ran away from the fire, his stomach turning as she disappeared between the trees.

He took a deep breath. Another. Finally, he whispered the words and felt himself transform.

The spell worked wonders, as always. He could tell because the tear-soaked face of the boy was slipping away from his mind, fear dissipating, all sensations distant like a voice drowned out by the wind. His thoughts solidified into a narrow, rigid corridor, no wavering, no doubt, and the sword became weightless in his hand. The cacophony of screams and cries shifted into distinguishable timbres, then words. He was ready.

Humans always made him shudder, both too fragile and too resilient, the most cruel, deceptive, and aggressive animals he knew. They hurt to kill, hurt more when kept alive. Only as his skin cooled, and blood rushed to his muscles, senses sharper than his blade, did he become the worst thing for miles around.

It should be obvious his path must not be crossed. And yet many chose to do so. It was a blur—the townspeople running, burning skeletons of buildings caving in, heavy wooden beams crushing nearby walls, the lonely wailing of an infant, a parade of black-clad soldiers, colourful fabrics stomped into the ground, the clamour growing louder.

Arran never stopped to count, never focused on their faces, just coordinated his movements, only cared enough to strike with precision, wasted but a moment staring at the thick layer of blood as it coagulated on his sword, dark red slowly rolling towards the handle. He pushed forwards, bypassed those he could, until he reached the gate.

As expected, that was a stupid, stupid thing to do.

A tight bunch of them looked up at him in unison —the whites of their eyes flashing, swords glimmering, feet shuffling—emerging from a cloud of smoke, drowning in the sickening stench of guts stretched thin across the cobbled road.

Arran recognised the body of the guard he'd seen that morning. His thick scar was not destined to heal. Green and silver flickered on the man's finger— a ring Arran was sure hadn't been there before. One eye was still open.

A thought sneaked into Arran's head. *I helped no one.* And then they charged.

They were only a few years older but shared none

of the stupid kid's vulnerabilities. Their armour was thick leather, expensive with a whiff of fresh oil, manoeuvres unconstrained, each advance thought through, measured, rehearsed. It made him smirk despite himself—a good job, professional, not creative, but solid enough.

They deflected most of his strikes with ease, but he was faster, the steel growing heavy in their hands. He was lucky, too. The castle wall was thick, street narrow. They couldn't attack him all at once, and he was getting them, one by one.

Some awkwardly waited their turn, hearts racing, breathing constrained, eyes darting back and forth, feet stepping back. Horrified. They thought he couldn't see, but he knew. He also knew there were too many of them, even for him.

The first cut was nothing, just warmth spilling under his shirt, some subdued tingling. The second one actually hurt, but he barely flinched, engrossed in the fight. His sword grazed the stone wall, sending sparks into the air. One man mouthed something incomprehensible, and raised his hand in a defensive moment, but Arran cut through it, not slowing down.

More footsteps echoed through the narrow street behind him, a tide rising.

He no longer paid attention to each time a blade slashed his skin. There was something humiliating about it—withdrawing, balancing both sides, struggling to turn in the cramped space, elbows brushing against the walls. It was obvious he was getting tired. He couldn't tell how much time had passed.

A taller figure emerged, stepping onto the last man Arran took down. He was older than the rest, clearly the leader, shoulders broad, only getting involved to finish him off.

Arran was happy to disappoint. He kicked the corpse under the soldier's feet, watched him lose his balance, and drove his sword straight into his face. He wrenched the blade up, splitting his head in two. Before anyone managed to respond, he slammed the fractured skull into a wall with a loud growl. As it went with a wet, crunching sound, he looked at the other men and smiled.

The perfect performance. Hyacinth would have been proud.

One of the soldiers slapped his hand onto a slimy stone and threw up. Thank god for him. The street filled with the stench of stomach acid and panicking youngsters. The one furthest back choked on his own breath, turned away and fled. The rest stood gaping, then followed on shaky legs.

Arran let out a crazed laugh, and took a few haggard breaths, pressing his hand onto the wound in his chest to slow down the bleeding. The one in his back was worse. He tied a rag around his waist, putting as much pressure on it as he could.

The thought of crossing the gate overwhelmed

him at first. Fuck hope for leading to the deepest of disappointments and coming with the worst of fears. Then he noticed how quiet it was, all noise distant and subdued. He expected many things, but not the deafening silence which came after the soldiers disappeared.

The huge, wooden door was broken to pieces and pried open. The barbican towered over him as he walked towards the abandoned tavern—a few bodies at the front, most likely trampled by the people escaping the building, one man leaning against the doorframe, head hanging.

Not a single living soul to be found.

But carried from afar—a hundred breaths, raised voices, and scratching like a bunch of desperate rats.

The *back gate*, he thought.

Passing through, years ago, he saw a raised doorway with wooden stairs—most likely removed by the soldiers now, a high fall. And yet.

He ran past deserted buildings, empty enclosures, and abandoned streets, until he reached a small square, a bell tower soaring above him.

The soldiers had rounded up the crowd. The last few guards struggled to shield the townspeople pushing towards the closed gate—a desperate force, a mass of bodies squeezed together in a feverish, suffocating dance. Their frenzy warmed the air, a wall of heat rising against the cold night, ice forming beneath Arran's feet.

The moment was familiar, but Arran shook off the thought.

Nobody paid attention to him, the few who managed to run were just brief gusts of wind on his face. So he stood there, taking it in, fear gripping his own heart, racing along with theirs. His shirt was soaked with blood, wet and clinging to his chest and back. He could no longer ignore the spell losing its hold on him. Dizziness crept in, the world swimming and wavering, pain throbbing sharper with each minute.

His thoughts were distracting, nagging, going round in circles, filled with paralysing visions and predictions. They insisted on adding everything up, leading to the same conclusions, fruitless.

He knew this was a trap before he even came. That was hardly the point.

It took all his strength to refocus on the crowd. He whispered another spell, and listened to them closely, then closer still. His mind travelled to the moments when Hyacinth was a natural presence, an easy thumping in his chest, the veins on his neck trembling to the beat, the smell of soap and fresh sweat. Arran's eyes watered, but he ignored that.

He blocked out the screams, the scraping of swords against bones, and listened for the heartbeats. They exploded in his ears like a hundred voices speaking at once. Each with its own pattern, the uneven pulsing, the mad, quickening pounding, multiplying. It was like untangling the threads of a spiderweb, fragile and ephemeral. But then it emerged—the familiar rhythm, panicked as it would be, just right.

He's here.

Arran caught it for a few tiny, hopeful seconds before it slipped away again, the deafening noise, a discordant murmur, the threads twisting and tangling in disarray. He took a shaky breath, and heard Hyacinth's heartbeat again, loud and clear.

Still here. Still here. Still here. Still here.

Thank fuck. Relief surged through him, a chill running down his spine, goosebumps tingling, eyes watering again. There was one thing left to do, so he did it, a tremble in his legs, but stable enough it seemed. He walked ahead. A few soldiers spotted him, but he was just one dark outline of a figure amongst many. It was no longer difficult to hold on, the sound pounding in his temples, strengthening with every second, guiding him.

The crowd grew denser as he neared the gate, until he was swimming through a sea of flesh, squeezing and pressing. The pain faded to a background hum. His hands plunged in between the mess of bodies, pulling them apart. He tried not to look closely, sorting through faces, searching, until he heard Hyacinth so close, his presence was overwhelming. He hesitated before pushing past the last man whose eyes were so vacant and clouded with panic, he barely noticed Arran in front of him.

And there he was, hair covered in ash, face pale and smeared in dirt. He blinked hard, disbelieving his own eyes.

Arran shook his head and shrugged, as if to say he was not sure this was real either. It was the first time he wanted to apologise, for letting him leave, for contributing nothing, and failing to do the one thing he was good for, protecting. He opened his mouth but there was no point in speaking.

They were drowning in the noise, people shifting around them.

Hyacinth didn't need an apology. His lips shook, he teared up, and smiled so brightly, eyes crinkling, his whole face lighting up, so out of place it almost made Arran believe they were elsewhere. It would be easy to believe that, even with the pressure against his back, the drops of blood rolling down his leg.

He wanted to. They both did—so much, they almost could.

Arran crossed the one last step separating them and slid his arms around him, pressing hard. The heartbeat in Hyacinth's temples thumped against his lips, whole body shaking.

The disparate screams, the skittering feet, all turned into a unified, continuous roar. The people surrounding them pressed on with a fresh force—a mess of elbows, shoulders and hands, a moving swarm, sharp bones and soft fat—until they could no longer separate, their chests pressed together so tightly it was beginning to hurt them both. Arran tried to stop the tide pushing them towards the gate, tripping over flesh stomped into the ground, slipping on the mud. It was in vain, and his strength was waning. He stopped fighting and held on to Hyacinth, both their hearts slowing despite it all, drowning out the noise, something almost like peace.

Hyacinth brushed his cheek against Arran's ear, hair tickling his temple, warm breath on his face, vivid against the crushing pressure of the panicking crowd, fingers sinking into the fabric of his shirt.

It was fine. Neither of them cared what happened next.

Chapter 2
The Art of Keeping Things Alive

irst, sunlight hit his closed eyelids—a pleasant sensation, somehow unexpected. Second, the breathing next to him was even and strong, his arms wrapped around a familiar shape. Third, his eyes watered for a split second before he got that under control. *Fuck.*

Arran was afraid to open his eyes and kill the illusion. He could swear there was soft bedding underneath them, a window cracked open, birds singing their morning song. The wooden floor above them was cracking—a tavern filled with people. *How the fuck?*

Hyacinth hooked his foot on Arran's calf, asleep, and yet encouraged by a hand on his back, pulling him closer. His linen shirt radiated warmth. The line of his spine was very real and rather bumpy. The pressure of his chest expanding and pushing against Arran's side was a fucking blessing. He shifted and Arran welcomed the extra weight against his ribs, an arm sprawled across his stomach.

Arran stirred in place. There was no pain, no constricting bandages, not even a trace of tiredness in his muscles, nothing. Hyacinth's heartbeat resonated through his whole body, so forceful Arran could barely stand it. And, as if to offer the final piece of evidence he was right there, and undeniably so, Hyacinth, most likely engrossed in a pleasant dream, let out a soft sigh right by Arran's ear.

Arran opened his eyes. Everything was there. Just as he imagined.

The wall opposite their bed stood vivid and clear —the wood panelling flooded with morning light, dust dancing in the air. A white horse watched them from its frame—eyes black and shiny, milky mane blowing in the painted wind.

Hyacinth's breathing changed. He jolted, surprise written all over him, and stared at Arran's face so close to his. "Um," he started, mouth opening and closing like a suffocating fish. "H—hey." He settled on a shy, confused smile, just to notice his arm lying across Arran's chest, blink a few times, and withdraw it with haste.

Arran didn't move an inch, still squeezing Hyacinth.

"I—ehm." Hyacinth pulled away to look at Arran's arm around his waist, as if he needed a visual confirmation. "I insisted last night but—" He paused. "I thought you didn't—" His breathing wavered.

"Wait, am I arguing against my own point here?" He chuckled, then noticed Arran's expression and his face fell. "Is s—something, I mean, are you... You look as if you saw a ghost. It's—well—it's a bit unsettling. Not that I'm complaining. It's just that, ehm—" He inhaled sharply, ready to continue, but a change in Arran made him fall silent.

Arran was smiling, breaths unusually deep. Either Hyacinth was going mad—not impossible under the circumstances—or Arran had tears in his eyes.

"I—" Hyacinth was running out of words. "I—I've never seen you that happy to hear me blabber on like an absolute idiot." He tittered. "Or is that moved? I've never seen you moved before. Which is actually quite weird, now that I think about it." He saw an actual tear roll down Arran's cheek. "Well, fuck. Um, are you —o—or is that? Does this mean you actually want to—"

Hyacinth shut his eyes for a second, embarrassed. "Shit. I was—I was much better at this when I was drunk." When he opened his eyes again, Arran was looking right back at him. "Listen, I never wanted to make you feel obligated to try, by no means. That would be quite sad. But you... It's almost like—" He couldn't finish, stunned by the realisation of what was about to happen, all signs already there.

Arran lifted his hand, still staring at Hyacinth with unusual intensity, eyes flickering with pure amazement. *Un-fucking-believable.* The smile on his face was becoming a permanent feature. Hyacinth suddenly got it. Arran wasn't moved, just relieved. It appeared as if something crucial had happened, something Hyacinth could not possibly understand. And yet, even ungraspable, it was there, and it changed everything.

"Fuck," Hyacinth summarised. His own eyes were beginning to burn. Arran's fingers grazed against his forehead, and ran through his hair just above his ear, sending goosebumps from his neck all the way down his spine, rendering him speechless.

Arran's eyes darted towards Hyacinth's lips, which were slightly open in sheer fucking disbelief, breath animated, perhaps more than before. Then, for real, not in Hyacinth's wildest dreams—as he had to clarify for himself, and repeatedly so—Arran leaned forward and pressed his lips against Hyacinth's with the confidence of a man who was, in fact, in full possession of his senses, however rattled.

Hyacinth's heart started beating so hard it hurt, his blood flow redirected with such haste, even he was surprised. In fact, his whole body went fucking berserk, like any bloody thing that has been starved for decades, and lived in constant anticipation, most likely would, to be fair. "Ar—" he tried. His last try to communicate failed, and he got pulled right back in, relenting, a self-assured tongue brushing against his own, diving deeper, turning the word into a groan.

Arran reached towards his neck, caressed his jaw, hands all over the fucking place, so fast and fervent it was hard to keep track, barely a moment to take a breath. If this was anyone else, Hyacinth would swear all this boldness must be hiding some profound insecurity, but that was not what this was—only persistent, disarming tenderness and unmistakable Arran-style dedication to the task, whatever "the task" might be.

This was by no means new.

There was Arran who'd spend hours sharpening and polishing a sword, brushes deceptively light, sparks flying, strength in each push so matter-of-fact, it was hard not to take it for granted. Only it felt different to Hyacinth, the same force applied to him, almost harsh, yet effortless, the uninhibited roughness which looked so controlled from the outside.

Then there was Arran waiting for his victim to emerge from some godforsaken gate with the moon high up in the sky, clouds drifting slowly, calm, a dark figure leaning against a stone wall, a stain of dark hair reflecting the gentle rays of light, motionless for hours, showing no signs of exhaustion, enduring more than anyone would, not a shadow of justified impatience. Relentless. And so he was, not a moment of doubt.

Finally, there was Arran fighting his opponents as if his life depended on it, even when it clearly didn't, because so few could compare.

And here he was again, on top of Hyacinth,

tackling the neglected, greedy beast he'd ignored for so long. He had been refusing to acknowledge this as even a remote possibility for years and years. But once he decided on something, there was no turning back. Hyacinth just happened to be directly involved. And he barely had the space to make a move—overpowered, at the very centre of the issue, both its subject and object, and yet, somehow, irrelevant.

Everything Arran did was familiar and alien at the same time. It was him, for sure—recognisable, more present than ever. And yet it couldn't have been. Because Hyacinth's best friend Arran, the Arran Hyacinth knew, would never. He simply would not. That meant two things. One, Hyacinth didn't know him as well as he thought—an unsettling realisation. And two, Arran in love was just Arran, the way he'd always been. That was it. All he could ever be.

Even before Hyacinth noticed the tension in his throat and pressure building in his chest, Arran responded to it. He slowed down, each touch like a whispered question—subtle, but the message was clear. They could have stopped then. But neither wanted this to fail.

The next kiss was almost too assertive. "We're doing this, for fuck's sake," Arran said, not using a single word. *Well, apparently so.*

He was pulling Hyacinth closer and closer, as if he wanted to break through his skin, squeeze in between his bones, and crawl inside him. He grabbed on to

Hyacinth's shirt, hands slipping underneath to pull it off, losing none of the impetus despite their momentary separation, diving in again, his stubble biting into Hyacinth's lips, whole body pushing him into the bedding with iron determination, the old bedframe crying murder.

Hyacinth whimpered and inhaled sharply when the friction became too much, warmth transforming into smothering heat. He pushed against pillows, fighting for breath.

Arran straightened up, face flushed. Something in him changed again. He ran his fingers down Hyacinth's neck, tracing his collarbones, and stopping at his chest, both palms frozen in place. The room turned quiet. And Arran just stared, motionless, mouth twitching.

Hyacinth stared back at him, self-conscious, his stomach dancing to the rhythm of his frenzied breathing under Arran's inquisitive gaze.

Arran traced a line along his breastbone, fingers gently digging in between the base of the ribs above his heart, caressing the light dip with misplaced reverence. He leaned down and kissed the spot, breath shaking. "Oh, god," his broken voice whispered into Hyacinth's skin.

The weight of Arran's emotions was crushing Hyacinth, so obvious and yet unreachable. He stared at the man cradling his chest, and felt left out, as if he was witnessing a conversation he was excluded from.

Arran stayed there, cheek pressed to Hyacinth's ribs, hands wrapped around his waist, squeezing so hard it was beginning to hurt. He shut his eyes and let the sound of Hyacinth's breath and heartbeat wash over him. After a moment Arran's muscles slacked. But he wasn't calm. Hyacinth could sense the nervous hum under his fingers as he ran them through Arran's black hair, stroking the sweaty scalp underneath.

"Arran?" Hyacinth swallowed hard, moved by a sudden display of whatever-the-fuck-this-was. "Did you have a bad dream or something?" There was an echo of an emotion, a distant impression like a word right at the tip of his tongue, a suffocating feeling he was desperate to push down. "Did you—"

"It was real." Arran was convinced but the memory already started to slip, as a dream would, and he held on, as if it was something precious, although it was anything but. The images, the sounds—drained, water dripping between his fingers. All that remained was the relief and the affection, both dislodged. Then there was the fear—vivid and present, relevant and raw.

"What was?" Hyacinth's voice resonated like a buzzing in his chest.

"Nothing. It's nothing."

Hyacinth laughed, stomach and chest jumping, forcing Arran to lift his head. "That's a—" He suppressed a nervous chuckle. "That's a fuckload of nothing we have here."

Arran blinked a few times and began to move away.

"N—no, I didn't mean to." Hyacinth sat up, grabbing onto Arran's shoulders, pulling on his shirt. "Don't do that. I—" It was silly, trying to wrestle, knowing first-hand how easy it was to shake him off. "Please, stay with me."

Arran turned to him, eyes bulging. "What did you say?"

"I—ehm." Hyacinth hesitated, suddenly ashamed of everything he felt. He licked his lips. It burned, skin inflamed. The cold gust of wind from the window made him shiver, and he reached for his shirt, the fabric sticking to his sweaty hand. The idea that Arran was the one who took it off of him was already ridiculous and distant, nothing more than a fever dream.

Arran just sat a few inches away and stared at him as if he was a puzzle to solve. He appeared more controlled now, more his usual self.

"Tell me what's going on," Hyacinth said.

The curtains rustled in the silence that followed.

Arran's mind was filled with flickering images and screams, with thoughts and conclusions he hoped he'd never reach. It was muddled but still there. Just as Hyacinth was. Right there. Clear as day. "We should go."

"What?" Hyacinth's mind was cloudy, and he was so undeniably aroused, whole body overwhelmed. He sat up and leaned against the headboard, cradling his knees. "You can't just—" But of course he could. That was the bloody problem. Hyacinth wiped his forehead, sweaty too, and took a deep breath. "Arran, listen—" It was humiliating—his tone pleading, emotions overflowing and impossible to ignore. "Just... consider me for a second."

"What do you think I'm doing?" His genuine question came off as belligerent. "I'm getting us out of here, so—"

"So what?"

"We need to go." Arran raised his voice, tone not to be questioned. "Now."

Hyacinth didn't move, just looked away, shoulders trembling.

Arran lost all impetus, hand reaching forward, then withdrawing again. "You—" he started, tone softening. "You get yourself ready. I'll pack us up." He didn't wait for an answer.

They were out of the door in no time, not a word exchanged, Hyacinth still buttoning up his shirt as they walked down the stairs, the uncomfortable creaking of the steps barely audible as the voices of the guests grew louder—not many, but low and assertive, soldiers most likely, a high, female laugh cutting in above the hum.

Hyacinth held onto the handrail, Arran's gaze burning into the back of his head. The tension was fucking unbearable. He turned around to say something, foot falling at an awkward angle at the edge at the last step, and he stumbled, outstretched hands landing on a sturdy man passing the stairs on the way to his table.

"S—sorry," Hyacinth stuttered. "I—" Not having much to add, he took a step back, bumping into Arran behind him.

The man was not pleased—a city guard, clad in black, armour a little worn. He took in the sight of them with a conceited grin, provoked before Hyacinth even realised he was staring at an inflamed scar on his cheek a second too long. Arran was looking too. The feeling of recognition was a tingling at the back of his mind, distracting.

"A cursed knight?" the man asked, brows raised. "What would your kind be doing here?"

"Working," Arran grumbled.

The guard's eyes lingered on Hyacinth and focused on his swollen lower lip, broken skin, light rash from the stubble. "Work, huh?" He nodded. "Hard times, for sure." A single step towards Hyacinth, perhaps just to see Arran respond, and he did, already following the movement, ready to intervene, proving his point. "Right."

Hyacinth was very aware of his messy hair, buttons not quite done up. It dawned on him that he was afraid, not of the stranger but of Arran's response. They were so bloody obvious, exactly what Arran would be worried about.

"We're just about to leave," Arran said, a threat merely implied in the tone.

It accomplished nothing. The man was still in their way.

"Richard! Leave them alone," a low, female voice called from a dark corner of the room while the blended ranks of soldiers and guards continued to converse undisturbed.

She approached them—a mess of thick, red locks, a long dress, and a scarf with shiny, golden thread hanging from her shoulders. There was a ring on each of her fingers, a blink of silver and emerald green as she pushed an unruly strand of hair behind her ear.

Hyacinth gazed at her with interest and Arran felt like letting out a loud sigh.

"I'm sorry, is he being a pain?" She put her hand on the guard's shoulder and leaned on him. "Don't worry. He's all bark and no bite. I refused him a hand reading and he's been whining like a little bitch ever since. Accounts for his sour mood." Her laugh was melodic but jumpy, coming off as nervous, although she clearly wasn't.

"She's just an annoying swindler who pretends to know shit," Richard said, loosening up a bit. "Why would I care what she has to say?"

"He cares a lot," she teased.

"Isn't that always a bad sign?" Arran asked.

"What?" Richard said without looking away from her.

"When a fortune-teller turns you down."

"Not always," she cut in. "People in this town don't inspire me, that's all. No matter how hard you try, there's not much to say." She shrugged and addressed Arran. "Would you like one?"

"For fuck's sake, Vadoma," Richard raised his voice.

"Stop that. I told you, you don't want to know."

"I don't want to know either." Arran pushed past Hyacinth, eyeing up the door.

"You should consider it," she insisted. "We're straddling two seasons right now. It's a time of change, a stormy transformation. Don't you feel like that's affecting you as well?"

"Not really." He motioned at Hyacinth to go.

Hyacinth's eyes widened. "I'd like a reading." He punctuated the words with a rebellious toss of his hair, already holding out his hand.

"Hyacinth," Arran tried, just to be ignored by everyone involved.

Vadoma looked pleased with herself and grabbed Hyacinth's hand with a smile, then turned it around, eyes darting between his face and palm, until they settled, her gaze shifting from interested to intrigued. "Oh, I've seen you before."

"We've never met, I'm quite sure. However, I am, in fact, an accomplished—"

"Yes, you'd think that," she muttered, more to herself than to him. "Very nice, intricate." Her fingers ran across the lines. "Actually talented. So sensitive."

"Oh, come on!" Richard appeared both annoyed and amused. "He is the closest to a famous actor this place has ever seen. You can do better."

"Extremely loving and permanently in love," she added.

"Artists do fuck around."

"Excuse me?" Hyacinth responded with outrage, objecting to the tone more so than the words.

"Richard!" Vadoma puffed up in pretend annoyance. "You don't believe me? Look here." She pulled Hyacinth's hand forward, surprising him. "See those?" She pointed to two lines at the top of his palm. "That's heart and head, so intertwined you can barely tell them apart."

Arran chuckled, attracting their attention. "Yeah, he does—" A quick look from Hyacinth made him stop. He cleared his throat, face neutral again.

She hummed to herself for a moment and addressed Hyacinth. "So many lives intercut with yours, but never for long. And then there's this one here, running parallel, but—" Her eyes narrowed. "So much heartbreak."

"My love life has been both successful and extremely prolific, thank you very much," Hyacinth snapped, but Arran could hear the crack in his voice. "I'm—"

"But that's beside the point," she interrupted him again. "Didn't you want to ask about the blackbird and your dreams?"

"What?" He was stunned for a second. "How do you—"

"It's what I do." She beamed, and Richard turned to her, unsettled. "You saw the bird's little wing twitch one last time, and the sight chilled you to the bone. Your time is running out." She nodded, and her eyes shone. "And then there's that square, the tower, the crowd, the suffocating heat flashing through your mind."

Hyacinth was speechless.

She stayed silent for a long time, then laughed, a light sound. "Sorry, just fucking with you. I was at the tavern."

"Yes, but how—" Hyacinth tried again.

"For fuck's sake." Arran rubbed his temples. "Let's go." He grabbed Hyacinth's elbow and started to pull him away.

"God, Arran, stop this." Hyacinth escaped his grip and rubbed his arm. "What the fuck is wrong with you?"

"Ehm—" Vadoma hesitated, but then her tone became comforting. "Please don't worry. Death omens are things of myths and legends. Birds are just birds—black, white, brown, or anything in between... They're all like any other normal, living creature. Occasionally, they die."

"Very reassuring," Hyacinth deadpanned.

"It's your turn." She reached for Arran's hand.

"You've got to be kidding me."

"Free of charge. And if you let me, I might consider giving Richard a chance after all."

Richard perked up and opened his mouth, but then closed it again.

"Why would I care about that?" Arran asked.

"Well, don't you?" She stared into his eyes with a spark of recognition.

"Stop this," he growled. "What do you know?"

"Your hand?"

He huffed with annoyance but let her look.

"You two are quite a pair." She motioned Richard to lean forward, and wrapped her fingers around Hyacinth's wrist, comparing the two palms. "See?"

"See what?" Richard asked.

"Isn't it obvious? Hyacinth here," she motioned towards his hand, "a complex net, so much overlap, intercutting, lines branching out... Even the lifeline breaks multiple times. It's a total mess, to be frank. While here," she lifted Arran's wrist, "it's like somebody chiseled him from marble. Straight lines, barely any nuance, so simple and pragmatic, a great fucking insurmountable gulf between head and heart."

"You need to look at our hands to figure that out?" Arran seemed amused.

"And yet," she continued, "look at their marriage lines, a perfect match." She nodded at Richard who suppressed a smile.

Arran glanced up at her, something between irritation and disbelief.

Hyacinth just seemed hurt and withdrew his arm. "You're right. Let's go."

"You told me, you can't match hands from two people," Richard said.

"That's true." She cracked up.

Hyacinth laughed, sounding a bit desperate. "Incredible."

"You've been running off his last performance and the stubble rash. What about that square?" Arran's tone was so indifferent, it surprised even him.

Both Hyacinth and Vadoma looked up with interest.

"What do you want to know?" She reached for his hand again.

"Do your worst."

"As you wish." She took a deep breath, fingers already drifting over the lines of his palm. "Hmmm..." Her head tilted in concentration. "There's a loss coming, an echo of something that already took place. It's like a rhythm stuck in your head—hands empty, then full, empty, then full again. There's an owl crying in the night. You heard it, both of you—a calling of darkness you crave to break through with light. But they are two sides of the same coin, at war, and the harder you try to save one, the more you tear them apart. And you're scared." She raised her brows at Arran. "Scared both of death and of life, scared of admitting both can be one. Perhaps there is no fight. Perhaps this trap is your home. It's almost spring now and, whether you want it or not, the flowers will bloom, the air will warm."

Arran's mouth twitched.

"There are shadows ahead of you, yes. Something will end, another thing will begin. But you're lucky. There's a way out for you."

"By 'you' do you mean us or me?" he asked.

Hyacinth turned towards him and stared, surprised.

"Do you mean us or me?" he repeated, ignoring Hyacinth.

"I don't know." She shook her head. "Sorry. I'm sorry. That was total gibberish, wasn't it?" She laughed and shivered.

Richard wrapped his arm around her waist, using the opportunity, then pulled her scarf more tightly around her. "Are you alright?"

"Yeah, sure, yeah." She didn't sound convinced at all, then smiled at him with genuine affection. "Eh... That's exactly how not to do it. Read the lines. Stop yourself from vomiting up random nonsense." She laughed again. "That's all I have."

Richard appeared relieved to see her return to normal. "Is it? I thought you promised me something."

"Ah, right." She rubbed her hands together. "Fine. Have it your way. If that's really what you want." She giggled, then took a glance at his outstretched palm. "Yes, yes." She nodded, deep in thought. "Just as I thought. You're going to die tonight, right by that gate." She straightened up and pointed in that approximate direction with dramatic emphasis.

"Vadoma!" He feigned shock and then giggled. "You really can't stop yourself."

"I really can't!" She laughed along with him.

"You're unbearable!"

"I know, I know."

Arran and Hyacinth stood there, the sound of frantic laughter growing louder. Finally, Hyacinth nudged Arran and they moved towards the door.

"See you both soon," Vadoma shouted after them. "Just remember to"—she suppressed a chuckle—"breathe." And then she laughed again.

The door closed behind them, shutting out the sound of her voice, and the reluctant warmth of the spring sun hit their faces, the winter chill hiding underneath.

Many people shuffled through the square to the sound of hooves on cobbled roads, straw still damp from the rainfall during the night, a dusting of ice sparkling in the light. Everything was so bloody calm and normal; they seemed out of place somehow.

"Creepy," Hyacinth started, determined not to reveal how unsettled he was. "What did she mean?"

"She wasn't making any sense." Arran shrugged,

moving ahead, feet carrying him towards the stables with unexpected haste.

"Yeah. And yet, you knew exactly what she was talking about," Hyacinth insisted, following along, noticing a few heads turning as they went. "There's plenty you're not telling me."

"If you say so," Arran murmured, uninterested. He was taking in the stables, the planks, and the solid stone foundations. Images of burning thatched roofs flickered in his mind, and he had to force himself to focus on the road in front of him. His jaw clenched, and for some inexplicable reason he worried something could be terribly wrong.

But no. There she was. He approached Beira, her head turning towards him with a light sway. "Hey," he whispered, smiling, already patting her neck.

She rested her muzzle on his shoulder, one ear turning to catch the sound of his voice.

"All good?"

She let out a quiet whinny in response.

Hyacinth shifted from one foot to the other while Arran began to brush Beira—all movements automatic, routine undisturbed. This continued until the coat was shiny and clear, hooves double checked for trapped stones. It was a gradual process, but Hyacinth was beginning to realise nothing might change. The thought came with a lump in his throat.

Once Arran carefully laid out a rug on her back and the saddle was in place, both girths fastened, he attached his bags and roamed through them, more focused than the activity required, digging through jars and vials, glass clinking.

The stables were quiet, just an occasional neigh from the horses, the sound of chewing on straw. A few people passed by talking, a casual conversation ringing in friendly tones, so measured and peaceful. It seemed unfair that people could talk like that.

Hyacinth started to pull on his sleeve, a loose thread rolling between his fingers. It was one of those rare occasions when words wouldn't come to him, and every thought made his eyes burn and throat squeeze until it was hard to speak. He'd rather get it all down on paper—written words didn't cause havoc at the least opportune moments. But no such luck this time.

Arran finally found what he was looking for, and faced him, expression neutral, eyes darting away from his. "Here." He handed him a little jar. "It will take down the redness."

Hyacinth blinked, confused.

"Take it." Arran pushed it into his hand. He noted Hyacinth's vacant expression. "For your lips," he clarified, already turning away.

"Oh," Hyacinth exclaimed. "Wow, ehm, r—right."

"It's just a salve. Use it." He fastened the bridle, hands busy adjusting straps, eyes set on Beira.

"Or what?" They both heard the emotions simmering beneath the words.

Arran flinched, but all Hyacinth could see was his

back, muscles dancing as he reattached the metal hooks. "Or we'll attract unwanted attention." His voice was calm, perhaps too much so. "As we did already."

Hyacinth took a deep breath. "Can you at least look at me when we talk?" It surprised him how combative it sounded.

An unreadable grunt was the only response.

"H—how does this somehow feel worse than when you had no interest at all?" Hyacinth raised his voice. "I can't even understand why—"

Arran's shoulders stilled. "For fuck's sake, do you have to?" He turned and faced him at last. "I knew that if I ever—"

"What? If you ever what?" No response. Of course not. "Arran, I need to know what's going on," Hyacinth pleaded, anger already making way for his bloody obvious affection. "It's clear where I stand. Don't use that against me."

"I'm not." Arran shrugged.

"Are you going to act like this never happened?"

"Is that what you think I'm doing? I just—"

"You just what? You don't think this requires some explanation?" He hated that they were too loud already, and Arran was paying extra attention to the entrance. "You do realise this is, uh... pretty important to me, right? Or is that not clear yet? Is this, in fact, insignificant, and I failed to realise?"

Arran shook his head, face tensing.

"What the fuck was that? Nothing, all this time. And now, suddenly—" He stopped for a few breaths. "You decide when, how, and why. I don't even get to know the reason?"

"Do you think I devised some elaborate plan to fuck with your head?" Arran's tone was not conciliatory at all, despite his best intentions. "I guarantee, I didn't."

"You do realise it was not accidental? Less a case of 'I tripped and my tongue fell into your mouth' and more 'I've been at it until you barely have a face.' Am I wrong here?"

"Do you want me to apologise for that?" he whispered, looking around as if worried if somebody might have heard.

"No. Fuck, no."

"Then what?"

"I want to know what it means."

"God, Hyacinth... It was a kiss, not a fucking love poem."

Hyacinth frowned, chest puffed a little. "Oh, please. It was more than a kiss."

"Fine, it was...fucking, not a...poem." Arran somehow managed to stumble on both words.

"Well, not quite."

"No, not quite."

"Not quite fucking, I mean."

Arran nodded, a corner of his lips twitching. "Yes, not quite." His eyes flickered with amusement, a prolonged gaze which made Hyacinth's stomach flutter.

Now it was Hyacinth looking around, making sure the coast was clear, his face already burning, heart thumping. He had not felt as much of a hormonal teenager since he actually was one. *And it's been a while*, he admitted with some reluctance.

He took a step forward and Arran stepped back. "What the fuck are you doing?"

"Shit." Hyacinth ran his hand through his hair, trying to control the shake in his fingers. Doing so, he noticed a man walking towards a horse in the stall next to Beira's.

The man nodded at them, then spent an inordinate amount of time preparing to go.

Minutes passed by, their eyes meeting, but never for long. Arran turned back to Beira. Her quiet huffs were calming to him, the softness of her coat under his hand. A feeling sneaked up on him. He chose not to call it "panic," although the situation was slipping out of his control.

"Safe travels," the man said, whistling as he led his horse out to the road.

"You too," Hyacinth called back, feeling like an absolute idiot for no particular reason. "Have a good one! You know, best of luck."

"Sure," the man responded, thrown off by Hyacinth's exaggerated enthusiasm.

"Can we just leave?" Arran whispered through

gritted teeth.

Hyacinth appeared unmoved. "Actually, there are other things I'd rather be doing, but sure." He chuckled, then licked his lips and instantly regretted that, hissing a bit.

Arran let out a frustrated grunt and opened the stall to let Beira out. "Use the salve and we can go."

"That's it?" Hyacinth held up the unfortunate jar.

"Yeah, that's it."

"Fine, of course." He pulled the cork with a loud pop. The smell was strong, herbal, and made his nose crinkle. "I'll just put this shit on my face and this whole morning will disappear."

"Stop being so bloody melodramatic."

"Here we go." He rubbed the salve all over his lips with unnecessary force. "All gone. Happy now?" His expression shifted from a confrontational to a grimace of excruciating pain. "Shit, shit, shit," he whined. "This burns like a motherfucker."

Arran held back a smile, looking at Hyacinth's failed attempts to remove the salve with his sleeve. "Yeah, it does." He closed the gap between them and grabbed Hyacinth's arms, pulling them away from his face. "But not for long. Just leave it. It'll pass."

It surprised them both when Hyacinth didn't attempt to wiggle his way out of his grasp, and Arran began stroking his arms where they had squeezed too hard before. And he was right. The burning eased, replaced by tingling, not entirely unpleasant.

Hyacinth suppressed the urge to lick his lips again, but was failing otherwise, already leaning ever so slightly towards Arran, eyes hazy.

"You don't give up, do you?" It wasn't really a question, and Arran sounded amused, maybe even flattered, who knew? He didn't push them apart, as Hyacinth expected, hands still in place. "I just don't want us to get into trouble."

"Well, you can't 'get me in trouble,' Arran, because I don't have a womb." Hyacinth's eyes bulged in response to his own words. "Sorry, that was a horrid joke. I do apologise. I really don't know what I was thinking."

Arran tried hard not to smile but failed.

Hyacinth couldn't help but notice that Arran's hands were moving up, fingers digging into the muscles of his shoulders, immensely distracting. "S— so about this morning. You can't dangle—" He looked disoriented for a second. "Wrong word, sorry."

"No, I—"

"I can't take the back and forth, alright?" Hyacinth's tone turned sincere. "I'm not trying to be difficult. I just can't." He paused but, in the meantime, reached towards Arran with caution, and sat his hands on his chest. The solid muscles under the thin shirt were really not helping. "Um..." His breath wavered.

Arran hummed, his smile growing wider, less interested in Hyacinth's words than the fact that it was so easy to turn him into a blubbering mess.

"What I'm trying to say is... You're either in or out." He let out a nervous laugh. "Fuck, it's just getting worse, isn't it? What I mean is... Just, please, don't make it any harder than it already is." He blinked. "God, what the fuck is wrong with me?" He took a deep, calming breath. "But do you? D—do you actually want to?"

"Hyacinth, please."

"When I asked, I didn't really expect—I mean, there was no way what I said would actually work, right? And yet—" His fingers brushed against Arran's side, hips tilting forward, eyes darting towards his lips again, the look transitioning from shy to smouldering.

Arran could barely believe this. It was a move he saw Hyacinth perform countless times at courts and in taverns, usually followed by a sound of a woman giggling. He definitely did not giggle, but Hyacinth's fingers did run up his spine as they usually would in those situations, leaving a sensitive trail behind. His mind seized, and he stilled, neck and ears burning.

"I was a little surprised and overwhelmed this morning." Hyacinth's posture was growing confident. "I wouldn't be now." He swallowed hard, and Arran could hear his heartbeat again, racing as he finally landed on the question. "Do you want to go upstairs again?"

"What?" Arran snapped, raising his voice. "Fuck." He huffed, letting his arms drop and stepping back.

"You, thinking with your cock. How am I surprised?" Hyacinth already looked so broken-hearted it wasn't even fair. "I said, a hundred fucking times, we have to go." He focused on the wall behind Hyacinth, hating the sight of him crumbling. "You're so caught up in your fragile fucking feelings, you're completely missing the only thing that matters right now."

"And what is that, Arran?" His voice was subdued. He cleaned his throat. "What is the only thing that matters right now?"

"I told you. Getting the fuck out of here."

"No, quite the opposite. You've been doing your best to not tell me a single fucking thing." Hyacinth was trying very hard to stay calm, to no avail. "Why do you want to leave?"

"There's an army coming."

"You said we're off track, the safest option."

"I was wrong."

"And how do you know that?"

Arran shook his head.

"No, how do you know?"

"I just know. Since when do you question me? Are you the expert now?"

"Why are you like this?" Hyacinth's resolve was failing, the upset clear in his voice.

"Because you're—" He stopped himself before he said something he'd regret, anger boiling in his stomach. "Because the moment I throw you a fucking bone, you're all over me, until I can't fucking breathe.

What the fuck was that? Do I look like a cheap whore? Or a fucking court maiden?" He didn't wait for an answer. "Nothing's enough, is it? What did you think would happen? I owe you a good fuck because I must finish what I started?"

"Arran, that's just so fucking unfair."

"So what the fuck did you expect instead? A handfasting ceremony?"

Hyacinth flinched and his eyes watered. Arran huffed with anger at himself, backing away. He wanted to say something comforting, anything to fix this, but imagined it would be misunderstood. He was so fucking worried about giving him any hope, just to squash it again, he said nothing at all.

At that moment, they both silently agreed it was better to keep this buried.

That could have been the worst possible way to handle this, Arran would be the first to admit. But at least they were on the move, Hyacinth walking next to him—shaken up, yes, but about to be far, far away from this place.

They walked beside Beira through the narrow, cobbled roads, passing merchants and townspeople who paid little attention, which was perfect, exactly as it should be. Arran caught glimpses of Hyacinth's face. His head was hanging, eyes fixed at the ground. But at least his lips were improving, swelling almost gone. What mattered was, regardless of how bad things got, there was still a way to get him back. It was safer not to wonder what "getting him back" would actually mean, or what it would change them to.

One step at a time.

Everything appeared as fine as it could be, until they reached the marketplace—a swarm of people ahead of them, the noise jarring. Hyacinth hesitated but didn't say a thing, confused by his own response, something almost like dread. Arran had to encourage Beira, trying to appease her with soothing words. Hearing his voice was enough to calm her down. This was hardly a challenge. And yet they lingered, unwilling to venture into the congested area around the stalls.

As the crowd swallowed them, Hyacinth became uneasy. The stench of his fear stood out against the sweaty background, the smelly straw, the sharp aroma of food they should have stopped for but didn't even consider. Arran was so focused on Hyacinth, he barely noticed he was affected too. The sight of the swaying shoulders and heads around him was making him queasy, as if he was out on the sea—a storm brewing, waves growing taller, a dull dizziness he did not anticipate.

They squeezed past a group of people by the flower stand, a blink of saturated yellows and greens soon blocked by a mass of bodies, clothes warm with sunshine, a few random pushes and shoves.

A girl wearing a green dress smiled—a twinkle of white, but Hyacinth barely noticed. As the tide of people rushing in between the stalls carried him forward, he gasped for air. He shook his head at Arran as if to tell him not to bother, then started to hyperventilate when bodies began to lodge between them, Arran's dark eyes disappearing amongst a stream of unfamiliar faces.

Arran held onto the reins, Beira moving ahead, and pushed through to grab Hyacinth's shoulder, making sure they wouldn't get separated, then tried to drag him away from the stalls. The whiff of meat was bad enough to turn his stomach—a sharp fragrance of spices burning at the back of his throat. Cut off from the wind and surrounded by people, the heat was oppressive, voices loud and sharp.

Hyacinth shook off Arran's hand, words indistinguishable as he pulled away. He walked ahead on unsteady legs, until he heard something like water rumbling, all sounds muffled, soon replaced by a loud screech. The world flooded with shiny waves of blue, green, and yellow, balance hard to maintain. He was no longer able to resist Arran wrapping his arm around his waist to lead him away from the mass of people, shapes blending with the movement, air stifling.

They finally escaped the press of bodies. A cool, fresh gust of wind hit their faces. Hyacinth breathed in, the air invigorating like a gulp of water after a drought. Beira made a fluttering sound, and positioned herself in front of them, as if trying to shelter them from the noise and the people flocking towards the sellers.

Arran moved them further away and didn't care much for who could see him holding Hyacinth up by the shoulders, then taking on his weight, and letting him rest. It was easier to just wrap him in a hug, leaning against a cold, stone wall. The line between trying to help and a desperate embrace grew thinner by the second.

A panicked hammering in Arran's chest refused to settle. But what mattered was that Hyacinth was calming down, his senses coming back to him, a hand wrapped around Arran's neck, a warm breath by his ear.

Minutes passed by, until it became hard to justify what they were doing. And maybe Arran took it too far, pulling Hyacinth closer still, until he looked up, staring at him with something almost like dismay.

He moved away, still agitated but steady on his legs. "What do you want?"

Arran hesitated. "I just want you to—" His mouth twitched. "I just want you safe." He swallowed hard, an echo of his morning emotions shining through. "I don't want you—" He closed his eyes for a second, then stared back at him. "God," he muttered, and looked away. "It doesn't matter."

"You know what?" Hyacinth snapped, flustered. "I think you've finally taught me not to want this. An impressive feat by any standards. I hope you're fucking proud."

Hyacinth lingered, as if waiting for something, anything, his look transitioning from anger to disappointment, until he gave up, and turned away, his back visible for some time amongst a colourful mix of strangers in a busy market. Arran didn't call after him when he still could, even though something told him he must. And the moment was gone.

Chapter 3

The End

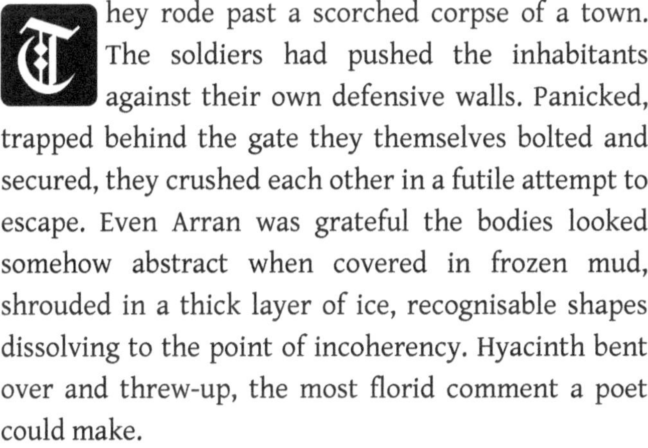hey rode past a scorched corpse of a town. The soldiers had pushed the inhabitants against their own defensive walls. Panicked, trapped behind the gate they themselves bolted and secured, they crushed each other in a futile attempt to escape. Even Arran was grateful the bodies looked somehow abstract when covered in frozen mud, shrouded in a thick layer of ice, recognisable shapes dissolving to the point of incoherency. Hyacinth bent over and threw-up, the most florid comment a poet could make.

Arran motioned him to go, but Hyacinth just gagged again.

When he straightened up, his face was ashen-white, lips colourless. "Sorry," he mumbled, trying to turn away from the sight. Only for some reason he couldn't—the outlines sharp in the cold, morning light. "Wait, let's—" He trailed off, and his eyes wandered. "There must be somebody still here."

"I doubt it," Arran said. "They were left to rot. Any survivors must have escaped."

Arran appreciated the crisp breeze interrupting the penetrating stench of death. The liquids soaking into rotting straw made the square stretching around them shine with ice crystals, rusty red snow filling the corners and preserved in the shadows. The bell tower stood above them, tall and imposing. The scattered clouds swimming behind its outline made the spire look as if it was floating through the pale, blue sky—a nauseating illusion.

When a hollow ringing announced the full hour, Hyacinth shivered. One of the windows in the tower was opened, and he could swear he saw a flicker of movement behind it, maybe just the curtain twitching with the wind. "You said no one stayed behind?"

Arran shrugged.

The stone buildings were unmoved and solid, but all living things had been crushed within. A single door led to the stairs of the tower, cracked open, the inside dark and impenetrable.

"Someone did try to bury them." Hyacinth pointed towards a line of bodies by the castle wall. They were laid out next to each other, a grim queue. "It seems as if—" He froze, and his heart accelerated.

Arran could not look away from the open door. "We should go in—"

"Wait," Hyacinth whispered and launched towards the wall.

Arran called after him, then followed with reluctance. "Fuck, why can't you—"

But then he saw it, Hyacinth staring at a familiar body contorted on the ground, his shoulders shaking, the stench of panic soaring above the overwhelming odour of rot and decay.

"That's what I was wearing yesterday." His voice rang hollow. He leaned down to look into his own eyes —wide open and empty, sky blue already clouded with white. It was his face, undeniably, turned to the side in a rigid, unnatural pose, cheeks caving in, arms stiff at his sides. "I'm—" He laughed, a frenzied sound. "That's ridiculous. That's completely—"

"No, I—" Arran searched the faces of the corpses at various stages of decomposition, features melting like wax. His eyes kept gravitating towards the terrifying, frozen shape at their feet. "No, that's not— no. That's not what happened. I was there."

Hyacinth turned to him. "Really? Then where are you now?"

Arran jolted awake and took a shuddering breath. He stared at the ceiling, still shrouded in the darkness of the night, disoriented. His awareness was slow to return, and even once it did, the details remained vague and distorted. His face itched, hair sticking to his sweaty skin, heartbeat agitated. The inn was quieter than before, just some muffled snoring in the room next to theirs, and the sound of birds chirping.

He hesitated before turning towards the window.

Nothing justified the fluttering of panic he carried over from the dream anymore. Hyacinth was there, facing away, a dark outline of his back raising and falling steadily, the space between them wider than before. Arran should have been relieved, but the sight seemed unreal, a painted image behind thick glass.

"Hyacinth." His voice was weak and raspy. He squeezed his eyes shut and took a couple deep breaths, but his muscles remained tense, chest tight. "Hy." A little louder this time. Only Hyacinth had gotten drunk before going to bed, and ridiculously so. As he put it, "neither a wild storm nor a marching army" would rip him out of "the sweet embrace of restful slumber."

Arran held out his hand to grab Hyacinth's shoulder but froze mid-stretch. What started as a passing thought was now a persistent one. Maybe this was still a dream, the figure ahead of him faceless, or monstrous, a trap set by his treacherous mind. But with a gentle pull Hyacinth rolled to his back, unsettled for a mere second before his face relaxed again—calm and asleep, a bit flushed, alive.

The night no longer threatened him with dark visions, and his heart settled into a calm rhythm, fear giving way to drowsy peacefulness, the shuffling of people downstairs sinking into the background. This time Arran rested close to Hyacinth, then closer still. Finally, he wrapped his arm around the sleeping shape beside him, leaning into the comfort and warmth.

They were fine.

Of all things, the gentle grasp of Arran's hand on his arm was what woke Hyacinth up. "All—alright?" he gasped.

"Yeah." Arran stayed still to make it easy for Hyacinth to drift away again.

"Mhm-mhm." He hummed, eyes shut, muscles relaxed. "Are we actually here?"

Arran tensed up at the question. "I don't know." A shiver ran down his spine. "Are we?"

Hyacinth wiggled until he was fully lodged in his arms. "I feel like you're hugging me. This must be a dream, a very vivid one. One where the world finally lives up to my expectations."

Arran smiled. "Yeah, it must be." He held him tighter, and stayed silent, hesitating. "I know I was harsh today. I didn't mean to—"

"Mm, yeah. No, it's fine." Hyacinth nodded. "It's difficult for you." He smiled. "Resisting the most desirable man you've ever met. Rejecting all the love and comfort. Refusing to settle in this safe haven, the only refuge from all encompassing loneliness and despair."

Arran fought the urge to smack the man. "You're fucking unbearable."

"Tell yourself whatever you need to, my friend."

In the encroaching quiet, Arran's thoughts began

to drift until he hit another memory, a vague recollection that made his eyes pop open again. "But I wouldn't have left you there," he started, louder than intended. "You have nothing to—" He couldn't push it out. It felt like a lie and his voice wavered. "You have nothing to fear."

But Hyacinth was already asleep again, unnervingly snug in his arms. And the night dragged on as if time had stopped.

At first, Arran couldn't escape the disturbing images haunting him. The corpse had Hyacinth's eyes, but the face was no longer recognisable, drifting away into oblivion, a blink in time. Trying to calm down, he forced himself to imagine a walk along a forest path— the soft ground underneath his feet, the surface malleable and loamy. Waves washed against the shore, a seagull called from afar, until the calm splashing of the sea transformed into something muffled and unfamiliar. He pushed back against the tide until all that remained was the gentle pulse underneath his fingers, a distant voice saying something he couldn't understand.

The blurry images solidified, until he was aware of Hyacinth walking beside him. They were going to a tavern, guided by the glow of the moon, most windows dark. Arran caught the name, The White Horse Inn, the sign worn down, paint crumbling. The door creaked as they entered, and a cold gust of wind followed them inside. The space was empty but for a lonely figure by the fireplace. No sound apart from the gentle crackling of burning wood and the howling of the storm brewing outside, windows rattling.

Vadoma was sitting by a table, head tilted down. She spun one of her rings, and Arran recognised the glimmer of green stone. He caught himself staring at her hunched shoulders, until Hyacinth threw a nervous look at him as if to urge him to do something. They appeared to have been trespassing, disturbing the unnatural peace of the place.

"What do you want?" she asked without looking up.

Arran took a few steps forward. "We saw something outside."

She hummed in response. "Yeah, quite a sight." She squeezed the ring between her fingers, the shimmering stone reflecting the light of the fire. "Quite a sight." Her lips warped into a bitter smile. "I was just beginning to like him."

"You barely knew him." Arran stated it as fact, surprising Hyacinth.

"Do you know her?" he asked.

"He's funny, this one." She chuckled. "If I could I'd also look away, but—well." Her shoulders twitched. "We're not all so lucky."

"Look away from what?" Hyacinth said.

She ignored him, addressing Arran instead. "I met Richard yesterday morning. But it's been a long time."

"How long?" Arran said.

"I don't know. Do you?" She shrugged. "He'll be back soon. It was just—just a bit worse this time, that's all. The harder I try, the more horrible it is, not quite sure why."

"Are we dead?" Hyacinth's voice was strained. "Are we actually dead?"

"Fuck, Hyacinth, stop that," Arran snapped. "This is not real."

"Is it not?" She straightened in her chair.

"No, it's not."

"I wouldn't be so sure. It does seem nonsensical, yes." She nodded and stared ahead in silence. The moment Arran wanted to say something, she spoke up again. "And yet, when visiting old battlefields, you can still hear the low buzzing of steel, the screams, the cracking of the fire on some evenings. And they are all still there, both sides, coming back to where it ended. Always one decision away from breaking the circle."

A memory nagged at Arran, but he couldn't place it.

"And yet, these are just stories, aren't they?" she said. "Ghost stories to horrify the children. Made up. No one in the wrong, no one to blame. As false as those rumours, the malicious whispers, which rustle behind your back and make Hyacinth's skin crawl."

"How do we get out?" Arran asked.

"Are you sure you want to?" she asked, unmoved.

Before he managed to respond with an outburst,

Arran noticed her eyes were focused on Hyacinth with meaningful persistence.

Hyacinth cleared his throat.

"What the fuck—" Arran stopped because his voice sounded wrong to him, too emotional for comfort. "What the fuck are you saying?"

She hummed again, staring ahead. "When a tragedy strikes, everything breaks like a mirror. You look at the shards and see tens of your own eyes looking back." She tilted her head and sent the ring spinning again. "You imagine what would have happened if you failed, or if you succeeded. You imagine it hard. Because that's all you can do. All the routes you could have taken. Gone for good." The ring settled on the table, and she covered it with her hand. "And yes, when you have nothing but lost chances— why not hold on to them, no matter the cost?"

"That's not helpful," Arran grumbled. "I'm trying to—"

"What are you trying to do, exactly?" she snapped. "Are you going to play stupid with me too? Are you going to pretend you don't know how this happened?"

"I don't."

Vadoma snorted with derision. "You know what it is about having a talent like yours? Very few can do this—warp time because they can't face the truth. It's not hard to point fingers when there are no alternatives."

"You're saying I did this?" Arran's question sounded genuine.

"Do you think I would have chosen to live in this liminal hell? To see him die a thousand times over?" Vadoma's eyes took on a wild shine. "We have to endure, not knowing when this will end, if ever. All these people, their lives, reduced to this. Nothing more than your puppets. Dragged into a cheap pantomime. One would imagine you'd abhor the idea."

"This must be a dream." Arran feigned confidence the best he could. "Must be. Otherwise, how would you know our conversations by heart?"

"Why do you know these conversations by heart?" she asked.

Arran tried to answer this question, for himself, if no-one else, but his thoughts were blurry, blending together, poisoned with misplaced grief. "I don't know."

"You're going over this—over and over again, because you think you can fix it, still, no matter what. But you can't. It's done. You can't change it. You, of all people, should know this trick cannot work."

Arran's head started to spin. "Of course, I know. I wouldn't—"

"But you did. And now you can't cope with the consequences, that's all. But we have to. We all have to, as long as you choose to bury your head in the sand."

"Consequences of what?" Hyacinth asked.

"Arran, of what?"

Arran turned towards Hyacinth and opened his mouth but didn't say a thing. Then he addressed her again. "Nothing happened. Not a bloody thing, you hear me?"

"Are you sure?" Her tone was so indifferent it hurt.

Arran flinched, not at all happy with Hyacinth's uncharacteristic silence. "I found him," he insisted, having to stop himself from pointing at the man. "I found him, and he was in one piece, just scared."

"He was, wasn't he?" She smiled. "Completely unharmed, after all that happened. It's almost—"

"Impossible," Hyacinth said, standing over his own corpse at the square, head shaking. The light was changing, the cold shades of the morning and the shimmer of ice, warming up as the sun lifted above the walls. "This can't—no, this can't be me."

"Stop staring." Arran wasn't quite sure if he was speaking to Hyacinth or himself. "This is not what it seems. It's a single possibility."

Hyacinth laughed. "Oh, that's fine. Why the fuck was I worried, then?"

"I'm trying to change this."

"We both are. Do you really think I haven't noticed, I—"

"I know." Arran nodded. "But you never remember."

"Yeah, and you never tell me."

Arran wasn't sure what to say. The quiet of the place was unbearable, just a distant song of birds—familiar, a call from another time.

"What if I am dead? D—did you—" Hyacinth's face was transfixed for a moment. "Did you cast the spell to bring me back? Is that what happened? Would you do that?" He paused, stunned. "But then I must be dead, for sure. Fuck, I don't even know what this means, I—" He touched his chest, feeling the heartbeat underneath his fingers, surprisingly steady under the circumstances. "I'm fine. I'm—"

"Listen—"

"No, you said this never worked. You said, and I quote, that the spell is 'pointless cruelty', 'a trap for the naive', 'the last resort of the—'" He stopped and stared at Arran as if he'd never seen him before "'—the desperate.'"

Arran tried to remember. None of this seemed real. "I'm sorry."

"Sorry?"

"Yes, I think I found you here, I must have. And I —somehow—"

"Somehow?" Hyacinth was at a breaking point, and his hands danced in the air, such a familiar sight, everything about him so normal, it broke Arran's heart. "You're talking as if this was an accident."

"I'll fix this. That's the only thing that matters. We're both still here."

"We're all fucking here." Hyacinth motioned at

the bodies around them. "Those stories—the stories we heard before coming to this town. It was a long time ago, when we found a place—a town that got attacked. We found all those people who crushed each other trying to reach the gate, do you remember? Is that when—"

"There is a way out."

"I felt so sorry for them, as sorry as I was sick." He tried to remember but the events were jumbled in his mind. "I wanted to let people know—to do something, anything. Almost as if I believed I could stop this from happening. Ridiculous. But I thought... Didn't I write a song about this?" He stopped and struggled to recall the words. "The cold grasp of the inescapable March," he sang under his breath, almost in a whisper. "I wrote it, just as we saw the first sign of the spring w—weeks ago. That's what I was signing before the blackbird. I was—I was—"

"There is a way out, Hy."

"How do you know?"

"There must be. I know there is. Wait." He squatted by Hyacinth's dead body and touched its chest, just an outstretched hand over the ribs, a moment of hesitation before he pressed down.

"What are you—"

Arran's hand met little resistance, the chest giving way as he pushed with a wet sound which made his guts squeeze, bile rising to his throat, the stench intensifying. "Shit."

"W—what? I'm—It's dead. And you're worried about a few broken ribs?"

"I was here." He looked up at Hyacinth. "I tried."

"But—" Hyacinth stopped at the sight of Arran's face suddenly as pale as his.

"Fuck." It all hit Arran at once. He froze for a few heartbeats, then took off, feet carrying him towards the labyrinthine, narrow streets he suddenly remembered with great clarity.

Hyacinth shuffled behind him as he manoeuvred from one bend to the other, every image falling back into place—Richard's body, the young soldiers lying by the gate, the scorched buildings standing bare in the light of day. And then he slowed down, his legs heavy as he reached a familiar shape sitting on the ground, back leaning against a wooden wall.

It looked much more natural than Hyacinth's corpse did, the posture surprisingly comfortable, head hanging down, dried blood all over the black hair, a stain on his shirt, eyes closed. Arran was not fond of clichés at the best of times, but couldn't stop thinking he appeared asleep, more at ease than he remembered himself being in a long time.

A gasp reached him from behind and Hyacinth jumped ahead, leaning towards Arran's still figure, as if he could help somehow. "Oh, n—no, no, no,' he repeated until the words melted into an incomprehensible sound. "You're just unconscious, aren't you? Exhausted, a little worn down." He searched for the pulse, pressing hard into Arran's neck, the old blood crumpling under his fingers, skin already rigid. "It must be—"

"Hy, stop that."

Hyacinth tried to find the damage that did the trick but couldn't. Even then he was cautious, as if worried he could cause him pain, still searching even when he was no longer sure what for. Finally, he turned to Arran. "What the fuck did you do?"

As if on cue, Arran's memories returned to him, so clear and present, it seemed impossible that he ever could have forgotten. "I removed the arrow. It pierced through my lung." The flood of impressions and feelings was overwhelming, but the facts were simple. "I left you in the tower. I was searching for Beira. I guess I...suffocated."

"What?" Hyacinth lifted himself to his feet and walked up to him, chest heaving. "You removed an arrow?"

Arran shrugged.

"First of all, a fucking arrow? Really?" He paused, eyes piercing through Arran. "I've seen you cut through arrows, breaking them into teeny-weeny splinters with a simple swing of your sword. In fact, I've seen you actually hit by an arrow once and acting like it's no bother at all. I've seen you tackle a dozen men and barely break a sweat." He leaned towards Arran until his breath hit his face. "And then you removed it? Even I know—" He paused again, realising what he was saying. "Even I know one shouldn't." His breathing was growing constricted at the mere thought of what this implied. "So. I am asking you. What the fuck happened here?"

Arran didn't want to think about it. The moment he stepped out of that tower knowing what he'd left behind, the whole world blurring, sound reaching him as if from behind a curtain, muffled and delayed... "I didn't care anymore. I was tired." That was the closest to an explanation he had. The piercing pain in his back was still fresh in his memory, almost immediate. The time it took stretched out in his mind. He sat here for god knew how long, breath shallow, then impossible, an agonising pressure in his chest, gasping like a drowning man. "I kept thinking—" He inhaled sharply. "What a waste."

"Well, my thoughts exactly." Hyacinth nodded. "How could you?"

"How could I what?"

"Do this to yourself."

"What the fuck was I supposed to do? Die slower?" He didn't like how hostile he sounded. "There was no one here who could help me."

Hyacinth swallowed hard. "I—" He hesitated, the sight of two Arrans too much to bear. "I know you can survive this. In fact, you can—and you should—just leave unharmed."

"What?"

"You don't have to die here. You don't have to *be*

here. You didn't have to—" His voice broke, but he licked his lips, cleared his throat and continued regardless. "And why would you? For me? Really?" He pointed at the body, his eyes watering. "That's not what either of us wants"

"You wanted me to come back for you."

"This is not what I asked for."

"But you asked for something."

He looked straight at Arran with a sad smile. "And what good did that ever do?"

Arran was taken aback, still unsure what Hyacinth could have remembered.

Hyacinth shook his head, gaze on the corpse. "I can't anymore, I'm sorry." He stepped back, nearly stumbling over a half-burned, broken beam behind him. He threw one last look at Arran before turning away.

"No, Hy, wait!"

And he did, his back visible against the colourful mix of strangers at the busy market, shoulders shaking. He stood still, the frenzy of movement in front of him a blur, sounds of a hundred conversations buzzing around them. It looked like he wanted to keep going, but was still dizzy, the smells from the stalls making his stomach turn.

Arran came closer. "Stay," he asked, lowering his voice.

Hyacinth turned around to face him. "Why?"

"You keep asking but—" Arran shrugged. "I don't

know what I want, or what the fuck this is."

Hyacinth managed a weak smile. "Those are... excellent reasons, for sure."

"I'm not leaving you here."

Hyacinth's heartbeat picked up and there was a glimmer of understanding in his eyes, face relaxed at last. "You say the most romantic things."

Arran grunted uncomfortably.

"Fine, I'll—" Hy looked down, embarrassed. "I'll stop that."

"Before all this started, you asked if we could go back to normal."

Hyacinth appeared lost as if "before this" told him nothing. "Did I?" He chuckled at his own confusion.

"Yeah, yeah, you did," Arran insisted, as if holding on to a thin thread. "You asked what it would take for us to go back to the way we were."

"And what did you say?"

"Come on, you must remember." Arran's helplessness was turning into anger.

"Arran—"

"Could we be friends again?" he tried. "Would that—"

Hyacinth's eyes flickered with hurt, but he blinked it away. "Yeah, sure." He confirmed with a reluctant nod.

"It's not fair."

"No, it's fine." He pulled on his sleeve with

nervous fingers and attempted a reassuring smile. "Where do you want to go?"

"Far from here."

After many awkward silences and a few hollow words, they settled into a comfortable stroll. Arran relished the feeling of walking along a forest path, the soft ground underneath his feet, the surface malleable and loamy. Shadows danced around them; small buds sprinkled on thin twigs. Light blinked in between the branches above their heads. Beira walked by their side, huffing from time to time. Her shiny coat looked lush in the sunshine.

It had been a while since they passed anyone, and there were no more houses in sight. The town was just another place they left behind. With every step, Arran grew freer and calmer, the nagging premonition he got whenever he glanced at Hyacinth dissipating.

Hy was fine, walking as he always did, a tiny bit slower than Arran would like, and his heartbeat was stable, tone casual. "What's the name of the next town over, again?"

"I don't remember. But we've been there before."

"When?" Hyacinth frowned, trawling his memories.

"Many years ago—a seaside place. It was the second—no, third time you were competing for that award you never win."

"Oh, you mean the Chalice of Honour, the top artistic achievement for any actor, awarded exclusively to the most eminent performers who distinguished themselves within the competitive—"

"Yes, that one."

"Ah, yeah." He smiled at the memory. "What was the line that got me all the applause?" The monologue was as clear in his mind as the day he performed it, but instead of quoting it, he cast a few fleeting glances at Arran. "Something about swans, wasn't it?"

"The swan song?" Arran didn't wait for a confirmation and, without much reflection, recalled the words. "There is a remarkable thing about swans. They teach us that the troubles of death should not grieve us; for in the very moment of dying they make a—"

"—a virtue of necessity and despise their sad fate in singing."

"Yeah, that's it. You made quite a show of it."

Hy glanced at Arran with a glint in his eye, then looked away with a boyish smirk. "Well, I'm glad you liked it."

"I didn't say that."

"You sure didn't," Hyacinth admitted with a wide grin. "I was pretty good, actually. I wish I had at least gotten a commendation, but hey... Lord what's-his-name paid a lofty sum for his sons to claim the main prizes, and I would never stoop so low as to—"

"Hy?"

"Mhm?" He stared at Arran. "Yeah, I don't remember the name of the town, no."

Arran grunted, somehow not surprised.

"However," Hyacinth started again. "What I do remember, and vividly so—"

"No."

"No? Fair enough. Not one of your best moments."

Arran snorted with amusement.

"Not that I don't appreciate the intention," Hyacinth added in haste.

"You should have stayed away from her."

"That—" Hyacinth seemed to lean towards agreement, but then shook his head. "That's still up for debate."

"The wife of the eldest councillor, of all people."

"Well... It was a spur of the moment thing." He nodded, then frowned. "At the very beginning, I mean. The subsequent stages definitely involved a lot of conscious decisions."

"What was it that they accused you of?"

"Arson?"

"Yeah, that's right. If they listened, I would have solved that for them."

"It was obviously that creepy boy with an extensive flint collection."

"Right? How did they miss that?"

"Wasn't he also related to the councillor somehow? A nephew, I think?"

"That explains it."

"It was, ehm—something."

"I'll never forget that bloody morning." Arran was somehow equal parts nostalgic and irritated. "I thought it was a dream, but no, just you screaming your lungs out from the other side of the fucking town."

"That's an exaggeration." Hyacinth seemed offended by any suggestion that his response was disproportionate. "You were close enough. I knew you'd hear me."

"I was thinking somebody was skinning you alive, get there—"

"—in minutes. Armour fully fastened and all."

"Did I have a choice?"

"Well..."

"Three soldiers are dragging you out of that ridiculous mansion of hers. You're in what? Your underpants?"

"My best ones, to be fair." Hyacinth puffed his chest with pride.

"Flushed and panting like you just ran a marathon."

Hyacinth's face brightened. "There was a reason I kept coming back."

"Her father is frothing at the mouth, her husband wants you dead, two of her children are crying, one laughing, she's pretending not to know you."

"Her father was there?" Hyacinth blinked, confused. "I have no recollection of that."

"It was easy to miss him in that gaping crowd."

"It wasn't all that bad," he said with conviction.

Hyacinth's tone was so comforting Arran almost agreed, but then turned to him, brows raised high. "They wanted you hanged the next morning."

"Yeah," he admitted with some reluctance. "That's true."

For a while they didn't say a word, and as the sandy, winding road brought them closer to the coast, they heard waves washing against the shore, a call of a seagull from afar.

"We should probably bypass this town," Arran concluded.

"Yeah, we probably should."

Arran nodded but kept walking ahead as before. "Back then, we shouldn't have stayed there as long as we did either."

"Why?"

"It gave you time to fall in love with her."

Hyacinth looked up, surprised. "Well, I always—"

"No, I've never seen you that heartbroken before."

"Maybe on other occasions I was hiding it better." Hyacinth shrugged.

"Despite all your bloody talents, you could never hide a thing."

Hyacinth glanced at him with interest but didn't respond. They kept on walking.

"I still can't believe you broke her nose," Hyacinth said, finally.

"It kept them busy. We wouldn't have gotten away otherwise."

Hyacinth bridled at his words. "You hated her."

"I disliked her."

"You hated her," Hyacinth insisted. "If her family wasn't there you would have strangled her with your bare hands."

"I'm pretty sure I was wearing gloves."

Hyacinth didn't want to find it funny but chuckled regardless. "Metaphorically speaking."

"She treated you worse than her poor servants. And you let her."

Hyacinth went quiet for a moment. A shadow of sadness passed over his face, soon replaced by forced cheerfulness. "It was a truly thrilling experience. Absolutely worth it. She simply didn't feel the same way I did."

"She wouldn't have minded seeing you swing on that rope."

"That's not true. She meant well. It wasn't her fault, it's just that—"

"She obviously never planned to—" Arran halted, and looked at Hyacinth, brows furrowed. "She was wasting your time and leading you on."

Hyacinth shrugged again. "I knew she was married when it started."

Arran muttered to himself, and resumed the walk, words indistinguishable.

"What did you say?" Hyacinth asked, rushing

after him.

"Where's your fucking self-respect?"

Hyacinth flinched, eyes lingering on his tense jaw. "Arran..." There was no response, but he seemed to be walking faster now. "Arran, I'm fine."

He let out an angry grunt, keeping up the pace.

"Do I really need to say it?" Hyacinth paused. "It's different."

"How?"

"I don't know... In all possible ways I can think of?"

"Really?" Arran raised his voice more than intended.

"You'd never—"

"For fuck's sake," Arran growled. "Don't justify me, like you justified her. I did cut you off before."

"Yes," he said in low tones, trying hard to remain calm. "I remember."

"That's better than this in-between state of—"

"Bullshit." Hyacinth raised his voice in return. "No, it's not. We were both miserable and I couldn't—" He paused. "We couldn't stay away."

"It's my fault, all this." Arran stopped walking and stared at Hyacinth with genuine concern. "Who's going to break my fucking nose when you need it, hm? Should I do it myself?"

"Now you're just being silly." Hyacinth moved closer, then hesitated. "Let's not—" He took a deep breath. "You're my closest friend and you do all you can, often more than you should. None of my relationships ever lasted a fraction of what—"

"I wonder why."

"Come the fuck on."

"Am I wrong?"

Hyacinth looked away and winced. "I don't know."

Arran just grunted again and resumed the walk.

"Regardless of what you might think, and whatever the outcome," Hyacinth's surprisingly faint voice reached him from behind, "you're the best thing that has ever happened to me."

He stopped again and faced him. "This is the exact kind of nonsense—" But he couldn't continue. There was something about the way Hyacinth was standing, the fact that he didn't even blink at his words—eyes wide open, an unmistakable combination of determination and care, so uniquely his. Somehow it reminded Arran of that moment in the crowd, the joy of seeing him again after being sure he was gone for good, the way he lit up, and all words faded.

Then he saw it, the movement in between the trees, a sound breaking through, a murmur of far-off chatter, the cracking of wood under the weight of many treading feet.

"Is that—" Arran started. "We shouldn't have reached the town yet."

"What?" Hyacinth appeared different somehow, expression neutral, breath calmer than before.

The light was lower and the weather cooler. The wind made Arran shiver. The feeling was familiar, a glimmer of something he already knew. Beira neighed, unsettled, and he patted her neck without thinking.

"We're here. Right on time too. I still need to change." Hyacinth launched ahead. "So, we'll stay at The White Horse Inn, but I need to be at the theatre an hour before sunset. You can inquire about jobs, if you need to—not that you need to, mind you. This will be decent pay for once. The room is on me. You don't have to be around for the performance, if you don't want to, of course, although I'd really like it if—"

"What the fuck are you talking about?"

"God, we're cranky today," Hyacinth teased. "I said you don't have to come."

Arran wanted to explain, but a gate emerged from between the trees, and he swallowed his words. The entrance was open, people pouring in and out, their movement mesmerising.

As they climbed the ramp, wooden boards flexing under Beira's hooves, the feeling of recognition grew stronger, then oppressive. Soon they emerged into a small square, which was teeming with life—hundreds of feet stepping on the straw lining the stones, a cavalcade of voices and sounds.

Arran knew exactly what he was about to see— the bell tower standing high above them. The scattered clouds swimming swiftly behind its dark outline made the spire look as if it was floating through the pale blue sky, a nauseating illusion.

"Arran... Hey, Arran?" Hyacinth tried.

Arran stood, motionless, the crowd washing over him. There was a small, dark shape lying on the ground by the castle wall, a blink in the gaps between the people bustling around the square. His pulse thumped in his neck, and he rushed ahead.

Hyacinth followed him, struggling to keep up and nearly running into a girl in a green dress, mumbling apologies with his eyes still firmly set on Arran's back. When he finally reached him again, Arran was leaning down.

Hyacinth followed his eyes and shuddered at the sight. "Hey," he spoke in soft tones. "It's just a bird." He put a gentle hand on his shoulder. "You alright?"

The blackbird's head was transfixed at an unnatural angle, one of the wings spread wide, bright yellow beak frozen open, the tiny eye reflective like a mirror.

"Hm?" Arran blinked a few times as if emerging from a deep sleep. "Yeah." His eyes were red and watery. "I'm not going to search for work. I'll stay with you when you prepare, and for the performance."

"S—sure."

"Could we go to the tavern after? I want to hear you sing."

Hyacinth laughed. "Come on, you're scaring me a

little."

"I need to hear your voice again." Arran held out his hand and grabbed Hyacinth's wrist, squeezing as if he was holding on to something that was about to fall.

"What's wrong?' Hyacinth fought hard to keep his tone casual, while Arran's fingers were biting into his skin hard enough to bruise. "I mean, clearly something is. What, though?"

"Nothing. It's nothing."

Hyacinth laughed, stomach and chest jumping, forcing Arran to lift his head. "That's a—" He suppressed a nervous chuckle. "That's a fuckload of nothing we have here."

Arran sat up and the bed dipped underneath his weight. He stared at the wooden walls, the painting of a white horse, its hooves suspended above the ground, blinked a few times, and began to move away.

"N—no, I didn't mean to." Hyacinth grabbed onto Arran's shoulders—helpless, pleading. "Don't do that." He pulled on his shirt. "Stay with me."

Arran turned to him, eyes bulging, breathing agitated again. "What did you say?"

And then the wall of heat hit him, back again—the disparate screams, tens of feet running, all melting into a unified, continuous roar. The sky was black. The people surrounding them pressed on with a fresh force—a mess of elbows, shoulders and hands, a moving swarm, sharp bones and soft fat, until they could no longer separate, their chests pressed together so tightly it was beginning to hurt them both.

Arran tried to stop the tide that pushed them towards the gate, tripping over flesh stomped into the ground, slipping on the mud. It was in vain, and his strength was waning. He stopped fighting and held on to Hyacinth, both their hearts slowing despite it all, drowning out the noise, something almost like peace.

Hyacinth stilled, then brushed his cheek against Arran's ear, hair tickling his temple, warm breath on his face, vivid against the crushing force of the panicking crowd, fingers sinking into the fabric of his shirt. As the pressure grew, his chest could barely expand, and his grasp was weakening. His body was becoming limp in Arran's arms.

"Hy?" he tried but struggled to break through the roar around them. He pushed harder, sparing no effort to make space for him, even for a single breath, straining to lift them up and failing, as the crowd dragged them ahead again, the ground moving from underneath their feet, extra weight pressing at Arran's back, nearly making them fall. "Stay with me," he managed to force out, his own breath running short.

The air was thick, ungraspable, moist, and stifling. And then it was not there at all.

The sounds became distant, and the world disappeared behind a curtain of blinking green and blue, the heat bitter and salty like swallowing a gulp of sweat. His lungs were heavy and immovable, a useless weight in his chest. The colours faded into black, first just at the edges, then the darkness engulfed the flickering faces, the dance of fabric and flesh in faint light. It took all his remaining strength to hold on.

Even once all his other senses failed him, Hy's pulse still thumped underneath his fingertips—frail, irregular. Time was slipping until he could no longer tell if it was passing at all.

"Move back," somebody's voice raised above the noise. "Move back."

The tide turned and Arran managed to catch a breath—a gust of refreshing wind travelling from spacious fields, a memory of long roads soaked in green and doused with sunshine. His vision cleared, and sounds became distinguishable again. He managed to reach above the sea of heads, and move to the side, catching a glimpse of the tower, sliding against the mass of bodies, drawn back each time he pulled forth.

The extra space made it harder to hold Hyacinth up, his body heavier than ever, sweaty, seams biting into him. He was barely breathing, but there was no time to dwell on that. The crowd was thickening again, the temporary relief soon forgotten. Arran found himself close, unbearably close to the edge of the square—the door to the tower visible, light in a solitary window doubling in his eyes. *Almost.* They were steps away.

Hyacinth's head fell to Arran's shoulder as he pushed forwards one last time, just a handful of people in front of them, and a few more scattered around. His heartbeat no longer resonated in Arran's temples, but it was there, at the border where their skin met, the light quiver in his neck.

And then it stopped.

Arran blinked and waited. There was nothing until he heard his own pulse racing in his ears, double the speed as if his heart was trying to beat for the both of them.

Something squeezed at his throat and his feet grew heavy. He should be rushing, not slowing down, he knew. Yet somehow, he could not move, his chest as tight as when they were still in the centre of the crowd, the world growing pale around him.

He closed his eyes, and it was all gone again. Instead, there was the warmth of sunlight hitting his eyelids, the breathing next to him, his arms wrapped around a familiar shape. Back once more—soft bedding underneath them, a window cracked open, birds singing. The old, wooden floor creaked, as if on cue, all the same.

Hyacinth hooked his foot on Arran's calf, still asleep, and Arran pulled him closer. His linen shirt radiated warmth. The line of his spine was rather bumpy. The pressure of his chest expanding and pushing against Arran's side was a fucking blessing.

He shifted and Arran welcomed the extra weight against his ribs, an arm sprawled across his stomach. There was no harm in letting himself enjoy this. So he did, trying and failing to calm down, but not for long.

Arran forced himself to remember the suffocating feeling, the thundering silence when the heartbeat stopped, the air heavy from smoke and panic. And he breathed it all in again. The dead weight in his arms was foreign, like it couldn't have been Hy. He had minutes, and little hope. But it was easier to carry him, because Arran's lungs were full, muscles regaining their strength.

He told himself it was just something he had to do, nothing more. Just the same as the moment before pushing a sword into a soldier, no space to think. He told himself many things. But none of what he did or thought made any difference.

Chapter 4
The Beginning

"**H**y?"

He jolted on the pillows, surprise written all over him, and stared at Arran's face so close to his. "Um," he started, mouth opening and closing like a suffocating fish. "H—hey." He settled on a shy, confused smile, just to notice his arm lying across Arran's chest, blink a few times, and withdraw it with haste.

"It's fine, stay."

Hyacinth lifted himself up and gave him a questioning look.

"Just... Go back to where you were." Arran paused, feeling presumptuous. "If you want."

"Really?"

Arran nodded, and in a blink Hyacinth's hand was back on his stomach, a foot hooked on his calf. He wiggled in his best attempt to get as close as possible, a stomach firmly glued to Arran's hip and a head nestled between his neck and shoulder. Arran smiled, and for a split second, a fraction of the tension in his muscles let up.

"Is the world ending?" Hyacinth said with complete seriousness.

"What?"

"Just asking."

Arran hummed. His hand found Hy's back again and began to slide up and down.

"Not that I'm complaining," Hyacinth added, glancing at Arran as if to make sure the hand was attached to the right man.

"Maybe it is ending, in a sense."

"It is?"

"Yeah." The lump formed in his throat again.

"I knew it."

Arran turned to him. "Did you?"

"Mhm." Hyacinth nodded. "I—I keep having this dream. Well, more like a freakish nightmare." His mind flashed with images and sounds, and an echo of panic made his heartbeat pick up a bit. "We're at the square, the one we passed on the way here. There's a sea of people and we're sinking into it. It's so persistent. I'm starting to suspect—"

"How much do you remember?"

"Only snippets. The suffocating heat. The moment it...stopped."

Arran grunted, words slipping away from him.

"The end, well—" He let out a breathless chuckle. "That part is quite striking." Hyacinth did his best to focus on the collage of vague recollections. "And there was a wooden beam."

"What?"

"Wooden beams and a pattern in between, not quite floral, like a weave. Lines, intertwined."

"When?"

"What do you mean?"

"It's not a dream."

Hyacinth went silent for a moment and his eyes watered. "It's not, isn't it? And this is not even the first time we've been here." A persistent, bitter aftertaste of rejection was welded to the moment in ways he couldn't explain.

"It's happening tonight."

"Oh." Hyacinth blinked hard a few times and took a deep breath. "Well, shit." It was both obvious and unbelievable, and hit him with the dizziness of an unsteady walk towards the ledge, the light-headedness that comes with looking down. He grabbed Arran's hand and squeezed.

Arran squeezed back without thinking.

Hyacinth cleared his throat. "Is there a—"

"No, I think we've tried it all."

"Yeah, well, that does sound like us, doesn't it?"

Arran grunted in agreement.

They were silent, the thoughts plaguing them too dark to express out loud.

"How bad was it for you?" Arran asked, at last.

Hyacinth hesitated, not eager to answer the

question, even for himself. "It is terrifying," he admitted with a nervous chuckle. "Slow. Gradual. Ehm... I never would have guessed that the dread right before it happens, that feeling of slipping away, comes with such indifference. For some reason, I always assumed it would be grander, but it really—It really does feel like nothing." He waited for the memory to drift away from him again, voice shifting. "But—"

"But what?"

"You give such excellent hugs."

Arran smacked his shoulder.

"Oi, what? It's true."

He just hummed in response, his mind stuck elsewhere, reluctantly returning to the moment when, carrying Hyacinth to the tower, he realised they might be too late. And the truth was, he knew they were. "I tried. I keep trying. But I fuck up every time. I fucked up so bad."

"None of this is your fault, Arran."

"All of it is," Arran grumbled with repressed anger. "I shouldn't have left you that day I saw you with Etain. You wanted to go with me. I don't know what the fuck I was thinking. And then, it never occurred to me, not until I heard rumours, asked around." The moment he found out, the memory he managed to hide, even from himself, was so vivid now —a striking isle of clarity amongst the fog of endless repetition. "I knew you were dead. I spoke to people who were there. But I had to make sure. And I did find you in that square. It took a while to find you, amongst all those bodies."

"Arran—"

"I told myself I had to see you to stop hoping. But I couldn't stop even once I did. All along, I thought I wouldn't be so stupid." His eyes started to burn. "I judged others for giving in, knew how pointless it was. I'm no better than—"

"Arran, I appreciate you trying."

"Do you?" Arran raised his voice. "Do you really? This is hell and you sure as fuck aren't leaving, not until I—" He wasn't sure what he'd have to do. When he thought about this happening to others he'd say "let go," but what he had in mind now was "give up". "I should have left you alone, I'm sorry."

"What the fuck are you apologising for?" Hy laughed, as if the idea was ridiculous, as if it was normal to feel spoiled by the gift of being trapped in an eternal nightmare. "You've done all of this for me. That's—"

"More than you expected?"

"More than anyone should expect. And—" He hesitated. "There's always plenty you'd do, but not— well, sometimes, you—"

"Sometimes? For fuck's sake, Hy. Do you ever learn?" It was unfair, but he held back long enough. "Could you face it, for once at least? It flattered me— all that admiration, all that attention, not what I'm used to, that's for sure. And you? You could have had anyone, but—" He stared at Hy for a moment, a fucking ball of hope and trust, so ready to find an excuse for him again. "A part of me liked stringing you along, fucking loved it. Poor thing, I thought, so in love. It never occurred to me. Not once. That I would go mad, if—"

Hy was about to cry, and it was really not fucking helping.

"As soon as you were gone," Arran continued, "it was bleeding fucking obvious. I used to think it was funny, how much you—" His voice broke, and it was tempting to end it there. "But I was the joke. I was the joke all along. You were beautiful. Even broken and mangled, you were—" He held back the tears, pushing down the memory, trying his hardest to focus on Hy as he was now. "I couldn't leave you there." And he wouldn't, still. Was that a weakness or a strength, he could no longer tell. "This is the one thing I can give you. The one thing no one else can. The best I can do, alright? I can make you relive the most painful moments of your life a million fucking times. You're welcome."

"Is that—" Hyacinth's brain grinded to a halt. "Are you trying to say that you actually want me? Is that you saying—"

"Is that what you got from this?" Arran felt like laughing.

"Am I wrong?"

"That's hardly the point."

"It is—it is the point, for me. Um…" Hyacinth looked like he was about to choke. "I—um,' he started again, tears beginning to flow, breath constricted. "I might need a moment."

"Oh, come on! What difference does that make?"

Hy laughed, and it was a wet and desperate sound. "Fuck you, Arran. You said we've tried everything. We sure as fuck didn't try that. I'd know. If you suddenly launched into a grand declaration of your feelings, I'd remember."

"You are unbelievable." Arran shook his head. "I just told you I've been treating you like shit and that we're done for."

"Far from it. Not even close to what you said. This is not the end. It's where we should have started. Can't you see that?" Hy moved away and stared at him with renewed determination. "We have to keep trying. We must, no matter what." He could picture the "no matter what" clearer than he wished—the stifling pressure of the crowd, the sharp pain that comes with the snap of bones, and the relentless pull of nothingness, the moments he could no longer tell who, or where, he was. And he was scared, but barely anything gave it away, just a note of sourness in his smell, so good at playing brave. "This is our chance."

The tension pressing at Arran's throat transformed into a slow flood of warmth he did not anticipate, but he shook it off. "There is no 'chance,'

Hy," Arran snapped, then realised he was scared too. Another moment was calling out to him, pulling with cruel persistence. "Your heart stops when we're almost out of the crowd, no matter how fast I go, which way I choose. And I get you into the tower. And I try. I try so bloody hard. Nothing. Not a single gasp." He shook his head. "You're gone by the time I get there."

"That must be—" Hyacinth hesitated. "Must be worse for you than it is for me."

"Me?" He let out a bitter laugh. "I did make this about me, didn't I?"

"Th—that's not what I meant."

"Yet that's what I did." He thought about Vadoma, her lonely figure hunched over the table in the dark expanse of The White Horse Inn. "I dragged so many people into this mess."

"What?" Hyacinth was finding all the various facets of Arran's guilt quite overwhelming. "You sure as fuck didn't start the war."

"No, but I got them stuck with us."

"Does that bother you?"

"They probably won't even remember when—" *if* "—we get out. It's not—" Arran heard the anger in his voice and stopped to consider the question—really consider it—digging in as deep as he could, finding nothing, and shook his head. "That's my problem. In the end, I didn't give a shit about anyone but you."

"Um." Hyacinth was at loss for words again, his

cheeks heating, half-overjoyed, how embarrassed by how desperate he was for that kind of confirmation. His heart was racing, and he grasped onto something to release the tension. "Not counting your mother."

Arran smirked, welcoming the distraction. "Not counting her."

"And Beira."

"Yes, Beira, obviously. I wasn't trying to—"

"No, I know," Hy interrupted, tone softening.

Arran turned serious. "I mean it."

"I know." Hy confirmed with an eager nod, and smiled, joy blooming in his chest.

"And yet, I've done fuck all to help you."

"Arran, you brought me back from the dead." Hy was on the verge of laughing again. "If that's not the most impressive thing one can do for someone else, I don't know what is."

"An eternal fucking optimist," Arran muttered under his breath. "You are nothing but a corpse in the middle of that fucking square."

"Am I?" He shifted in Arran's embrace, bolder, moving closer, breath running short for reasons other than fear. "Say whatever you want, but I'm feeling very much alive."

"Yes, I can tell." Arran smiled despite himself. "Not too bothered, are you?"

"I don't think—" He stopped with a huff. "This can't be hopeless. And now that we both know what happened—happens—that must change something."

"God, how many times—"

"No, you can't know for sure," he said, as certain, as if he did. "And even if—even so, the last thing I want—" He stared at Arran, eyes glassy. "The last thing I want to feel right now is despair."

Arran hummed to himself. "We can do better than despair." He wound his arms around Hy's waist, fingers digging into his hips, pulling him closer.

And that was enough of a provocation. Hyacinth leaned in and caught Arran's lips, arms wrapping around him, and drawing him in much deeper. His smell shifted from sour to musky and sweet. Hyacinth's pulse resonated through Arran's bones, heart pounding in his ears as their chests pressed against each other again.

As Arran's fingers got trapped behind Hyacinth's waistband, the fabric close-fitting and inflexible, Hyacinth let out a strangled sound, wiggling, as if he was hoping he could shed his clothes that way. Arran pulled on the drawstring, the material slacking, still leaving a line of intact ties underneath. He smiled and palmed him through the fabric. A long line of small, wooden buttons slid in between his fingers. He felt Hyacinth lean in, and heard him moan right by his ear, a puff of air tickling his skin.

"Don't get excited," Arran whispered into his neck. "These buttons will take time."

Hyacinth suppressed a laugh. "I can be patient," he said, his tone suggesting he was anything but.

But it didn't take long at all.

It was hard to believe and appeared much more like a fantasy than reality to Hyacinth's feverish mind. He would be the first to admit that his imagination had drifted a thousand times, recontextualising Arran's attributes, weaving them into so many desirable scenarios with dedication, love, and care.

Oh, how Arran resisted. So precious about how his strength, patience, and all-or-nothing attitude was applied, how far it travelled, even in Hyacinth's dreams. Even there, where Hyacinth was supposed to be in control, Arran would refuse to say the words he yearned to hear, would smile with derision in response to his affection, turning away, disinterested to the core.

Yet, separated into smaller, manageable components—just a displaced hand, a breath on Hyacinth's neck, a low hum in his ear, a single leg pushed in between his, leading to a bit more, step by step—he relented. Imaginary Arran could handle that, to a point. It nearly worked. And then it worked a little better, and better still. Then it became habitual, routine, exactly right every single time. Fucking perfect. Almost enough.

That's as far as this could ever go. Hyacinth was certain. And yet, he was wrong. He caught himself running his fingers through the black hair, following the movement, the tide slowly rising and falling. The pace picked up, scattered dark strands tickling his thighs, his heels digging into Arran's back, muscles dancing underneath—a steady rhythm, a relentless fluctuation, waves of pleasure rolling over him, the heat building up and up, until it became unbearable.

Arran could feel Hyacinth transforming—the lightest spasms, drops of sweat building on his skin, muscles contracting, breath shallow, breaking at shorter and shorter intervals, heartbeat wild. For reasons he couldn't explain, as he took Hyacinth further and further apart, he thought about their future, the days ahead they could never reach, the leaves unwinding under a gentle drizzle of spring rain, flowers bursting into full bloom. It seemed obvious, like something that was never out of their grasp. And just as Hyacinth stilled, breath frozen at an inhale, about to give in, Arran stopped. Time was running out, the moment escaping him.

"I'll find a way," was the last thing he managed to say, not believing that for a second, right before he heard the roar of the crowd behind them, Hyacinth's weight leaning on him again.

Arran still stood there, at the edge of the damn square, wasting precious seconds. That initial lick of panic was distant and faint in comparison to the intense regret taking its place, a painful twist in his gut, blood whooshing in his ears.

A few people ran past them. Arran walked ahead. The feverish madness of muffled cries and stomping feet grew louder, but Hyacinth's body was quiet—a hollow vessel, a vacant room filled with personal trinkets, bedding turned over, the armchair still warm, so full of the person who left mere moments ago.

It didn't take long to get to the tower and Arran kicked in the door with no difficulty, Hyacinth's head heavy on his shoulder. The staircase appeared endless, the climb went on and on, but he knew where to go from all the times they had been there before—imagined or real. Whoever was there before left in haste—the door to the chamber open wide, a lantern, still burning, stood on a small oak coffer in the corner.

The light flickered when Arran set Hyacinth down on a long table, lowered him down with care, as if he could still complain about being thrown around like a rag doll.

Lifeless, laying on a slab, he did look like a doll, an expensive one. His layered, heavy silk clothes—all padding, ties, pins, and laces—were impenetrable. Birch toggle buttons—oblong-shaped and sizable— were running all the way from his tall collar to his breeches, each sitting in a flowery nest of velvet.

"For fuck's sake, Hy," Arran whispered. He undid the first button, the awkward shape slipping from his sweaty fingers. Slow. Too slow. He shook his head and pulled on the fabric with full force, buttons flying, and revealing a boned, laced garment underneath, the binding wrapped tight. "It's like you don't want to breathe."

He grabbed a knife from his belt and cut through the lacing—a long, precise incision like gutting a fish. They were down to a linen shirt. *Good enough.*

Arran traced a line along Hyacinth's breastbone, fingers gently digging in between the base of the ribs above his heart, then pushed hard into his chest, catching a good rhythm. He squeezed his eyes shut, feeling the cartilage between the ribs loosening up, sternum strained but flexible, pushing back against his hands. It took some effort to block out the memory of the dead body at the square, chest squashy and fallen in. "Come on," he said, then chastised himself. A waste of breath, so stupid, why would he— "Come on, Hy."

He lifted Hyacinth's chin. His lips were colourless and cold, something Arran tried to ignore as he pushed his breath into Hyacinth's lungs. Operating his body in his absence was a weird intrusion—making him inhale, pushing the blood through his body, limbs pliant under his fingers, like handling a string puppet. But it was a relief to feel his lungs expand again, chest rising under his hand, so normal, Arran could almost imagine it was of Hy's own volition—an illusion of life, his last, and most important, performance.

Arran took in as much air as he could. The smell was unbearable—woody and ambery, sweet and earthy, musky, velvety and smooth, overwhelming and primal. It was like a scream in the night—bells ringing, a silent plea for help, an admission of defeat.

Hyacinth smelled and felt like a dead man, any dead man, his features fading, distinctiveness dissolving into nothingness.

From then on, time stood still.

Perhaps it would be less painful to imagine this was somebody else. Only if it was, Arran wouldn't have done this in the first place, or would have given up already, perhaps long ago. He hated admitting it, but he was slowing down, muscles no longer just stiff, but hurting. The cuts in his back were impossible to ignore, scabs breaking with every movement, dry blood itching.

A quiet whisper of doubt grew louder in his mind. "He's dead. He's dead. He's dead," it repeated with every push. A hundred fucking times per minute, until words melted into a blur of sounds and letters. "He's fucking dead. What the fuck are you doing?" But he didn't stop. It was much easier to continue than admit they were done.

Then came the nausea, the salty taste of sweat on his lips, drips making his face itch, hair tickling his cheeks, the breathlessness which made it hard for him to keep the rhythm. Hyacinth's chest was not rising as high or as steadily as before. The uneven pace felt desperate, worse, useless, irrational, fucking stupid, pointless, naive, doomed to fail.

He needed a moment. A break was a mistake. A break was the only option. He stopped. Hyacinth was completely motionless, limp, and hopeless.

"If you're s—so—sure—we can get outo—f here—alive—then fucking breathe." Arran was not quite able to follow his own advice. His mouth was so dry, his lips were flaking, lungs burning. He tried again, Hyacinth's chest suddenly unwilling to lift. And again. All that came out was broken panting, clammy fingers sticking to Hyacinth's cheeks.

He couldn't do it.

For a while he just sat there, resting, jaw clenched, eyes watering, not only from exertion.

Fuck. And back again. Not sure how, but there was a new burst of energy, a growing indifference to his own weariness, movements persistent and automatic, all emotions distant, the sound of bones popping muffled in his ears. Hy's head was tapping against the table—a thump almost like a heartbeat, the pushes stronger and deeper. It was doable. He could go on.

He pushed again, much harder this time, with hope, and he heard the ribs crack, hand going further in than intended, and his shoulder seized in a cramp.

He stopped, pain shooting through him. That was it. *That's it.* He stretched his back and strained neck, muscles tensing, then relaxed. The fibres twitched, the agony still clawing at him. *Fuck it, makes no difference. It's too late.* And for a moment he was numb. No feelings, just his heart thumping in his neck, breathing so frantic it hurt, a burning at the back of his throat, tongue stuck to the roof of his mouth, a throbbing ache in his upper back, nothing more.

As soon as the haze of exhaustion subdued, he grabbed Hyacinth's hand, his breath broken for good. He weaved their fingers together while they were still flexible enough to move.

A random spasm made Hyacinth's hand twitch, almost like an attempt to reciprocate, and Arran just stared, stunned.

It hit him then, his shoulders shaking, a penetrating sting in his chest. He stared at the wall in front of him, afraid to look at Hyacinth's pale face. There was something, still, something he promised himself to remember. The memory came to him, and without hurry, unsure if he was ready for reality to disappoint, he looked up.

There was a wooden beam. Above their heads, right in front of Hy's closed eyes. Many wooden beams, to be precise, with a pattern in between, not quite floral, like a weave. Lines, intertwined. Arran felt like he was choking.

"Hy?"

"Yeah?" he said, hair scattered on the pillow, face bathed in soft light falling through a tavern window. "Yeah, why did you stop? I—" He chucked, breathless. "I was getting—I was—"

"Were you?" Arran's relief was too overwhelming to hide.

"Y—yeah. How the fuck is that surprising?"

Arran let go of his hand and pushed down on his chest again, the feeling of the fractured rib under his palm impossible to ignore, bones snapping.

Hyacinth grabbed onto Arran's shoulders, fingers biting into his muscles, then sliding down his back. "C —come on, I won't break."

Arran pressed on Hyacinth's ribs—harder, and again, his face wet from tears. "Come on," he whispered, his own chest hurting as he tried again. "Come on, Hy."

"D—don't stop," Hyacinth kept repeating, although there clearly was no need to—face flushed, pillow riding up towards the bed frame. "Don't stop." His hand quivered, breathing accelerated, until all air escaped his lungs at once, a sense of euphoria spilling in his chest, all pain gone in an ecstatic second, muscles spasming, fear wiped out.

Bliss arrived with a gasp, then another, and another. His heartbeat, erratic at first, grew stable in Arran's ears. Hyacinth was barely aware of Arran holding him through it, feeling every bit of the tremor, savouring the sensation of him breathing into his ear.

"God," Hyacinth groaned, the word a smothered whisper. The pain in his torso was agonising, respiration short and shallow. The ceiling danced in front of his eyes, wooden beams blurry, then regaining their shape. "F—fuck."

"Yeah." Arran nodded, squeezing Hyacinth's hand again. An uncontrollable smile spilled all over his face as he felt him clutch it in return. "All there?"

"Y—yeah. I—th—think—" Hyacinth huffed, struggling, tones hushed almost to oblivion.

Arran was breathing easier, and Hyacinth's heartbeat was reassuringly strong, an assertive thumping in his temples. "Good," he managed to say. He pushed himself up and towered over Hy—hair messy, eyes stinging, and wiped off the tears, still flowing somehow.

"You—look—" Hyacinth tried to turn his head but couldn't, words intercut with groans, his whole body stiff and tingling. "You—look—I—like—I—di—died." He chuckled, wincing with each pause.

"You did."

"Quite—fla—flattering—really." The mix of smugness and suffering was something to behold.

"Yeah, maybe don't talk." Arran's voice sounded unusually affectionate in his own ears.

The noise of the struggle outside began to come back to him. The room was stilted and stuffy, dust dancing in the flickering light of the lantern. But it was nothing like the nightmarish space he remembered—not empty, but filled with Hyacinth's frantic panting, overflowing with his sighs and muffled sobs.

And, of course, Hyacinth did not stop talking. "N—no— air—here," he said.

"Yeah, wait." He let go of Hyacinth's hand—apprehensive, an inkling of uneasiness as Hyacinth's fingers slipped out of his. Ridiculous. The window was only a few steps away.

The lock gave way, and a gust of wind hit his face —perfect. He looked ahead, ignoring the sound, not looking down, already knowing what was there.

The window on the other side opened to the castle gardens, not a human in sight, only winding paths, and hedge labyrinths. Arran stilled, staring at the cherry trees in bloom—a flood of white blossoms, no leaves yet. The air was perfused with the floral scent, rich and creamy like vanilla, sweet as roses, heavy and warm—warmer than expected. The sky, still dark and tranquil, brightened at the horizon, tinged with the orange hues of the rising sun.

As he moved back, a blackbird surprised him, darting in to land on the ledge, head tilting with interest, beak opening and closing, its high-pitched vibrato echoing through the room. A tiny, reflective, black eye in a sunflower-yellow frame lingered on him before the bird surged up, wings fluttering.

Arran's chest clenched. He stood, dazed and overwhelmed, the wind shifting to cooler again, the space fresh and airy, at last.

The light outside was too faint for human eyes, nothing more than a thin gleaming line announcing the day to come, but it was vivid to him, illuminating the room, surrounding Hyacinth with a faint glow he could not yet see.

"We have to wait a bit longer," Arran said, feeling a bit silly as he held onto Hy's hand again. "Then I'll go and find Beira. I'll get you something for the pain."

"N—no, do—don't—don't leave."

"I'm not leaving, I'm—"

"L—let's stay now, go together. When it's s—safe."

"You sure?"

"Mhm."

"Of course, you are," Arran whispered, emotions swelling in his throat.

"Y—yeah."

Arran brushed a few strands of filthy blonde hair away from Hyacinth's sweaty forehead, and stared in pure amazement at the colours returning—cheeks blushed, eyes clear and bright, blue in full bloom, life forcing its way back in. And the warmth engulfed him too— persistent, impossible to shake off, demanding to be voiced. "I love you," he admitted with great relief, breath catching.

Hyacinth took a few gulps of air and huffed a few times. He choked and cleared his throat, trying to speak, but kept getting caught in a bout of rapid gasps. Finally, he managed to force out, "What?"

Acknowledgements

Jennifer Moffatt is the heart of this novella and the reason it exists. While writing might seem like a solitary activity, it has always felt like a dialogue to me, and Jenn has been the best conversation partner. She has supported me for years, and spent innumerable hours inspiring, proofreading, and refining my work. This book is dedicated to her.

Nate Ragolia has been a source of joy since he accepted this novella for publication. He is the kindest, the most enthusiastic person, and he has been accommodating, hardworking, and helpful—the dream editor throughout. It is rare to be respected, appreciated, and given the space to shape and improve one's work. This collaboration has been an absolute pleasure.

As I developed this story, Melania Ortiz Alvarez de la Campa and Yannick Lucian Lapetta worked with me to make illustrations. The novella went through many permutations and is a different beast now, but the awe-inspiring creativity of those two artists remains a core part of it. Yannick, who is a specialist in zoology, also helped to develop Beira into a character of her own and taught me plenty about horses.

Nani Albarello is the medical expert behind this text. She is impressively well-read, intellectually curious and inquisitive, has an amazing eye for details, and a precise and informed sense of how things look, smell, and feel—from resuscitations, to fabrics, to the mediaeval diet. I am immensely grateful to her. All the remaining inaccuracies, and artistic liberties, are mine.

Justine Dessed is such a talented writer. Before I started drafting, I was proofreading her work and admired the way she captured the dance-like rhythm of everyday interactions, a poetic depth of feelings, and a kind of melancholic beauty. She inspired me to search for my own ways to reach similar qualities and feed them into my novella.

I would also like to extend the warmest thanks to Rosie and Ali Coyle for their generous response to the first draft and their encouragement.

Seb Doubinsky somehow found me by wading through the confusing mess of social media. A single tweet from him, praising my story in *Every Day Fiction* (ironically enough, called "One Chance in a Million"), led to you holding this novella in your hands. I greatly appreciate Seb's excellent writing, and his generosity. He always finds time to elevate fellow writers and turns this competitive neoliberal hellscape into a collegial environment. It is an honour to have such a well-established, talented, and versatile writer in my corner.

I started writing this novella in March 2021 and death was on my mind. I didn't yet know that my grandfather was about to pass away, but I could sense it, and I was desperate to break through that darkness with some hope. He was a remarkable, warm, and generous man who lived through the horrors of war and emerged without an ounce of bitterness or cynicism in his heart. An electrician, mechanic, and a builder by trade, once age took away his ability to help others, he spent long hours dreaming up scenarios in which he was able to fix things once again. The imaginary space where the impossible happens is a land we will always share.

About the Author

Hana Carolina (she/her) is a pseudonym of an Edinburgh-based creative and academic writer. In love with the gothic atmosphere of Scotland, she moved out of Poland as a teen and now balances her old, tired Polish identity with a conflicted mix of Scottish and British. She studied literature, film, and television for many years, and wrote a PhD thesis about the psychology of audience engagement with fictional characters. Hana has worked as a tutor, interpreter, and researcher, all while publishing academically and writing dark stories about horrible people...who on occasion end up involved in elaborate, tragically romantic scenarios.

About the Publishers

Nate Ragolia is a lifelong lover of science fiction and its power to imagine worlds more hopeful and inclusive than the real one. His first book, *There You Feel Free*, was published by 1888's Black Hill Press in 2015. Spaceboy Books reissued it in 2021. He's also the author of *The Retroactivist* (2017). His most recent book, *One Person Can't Make a Difference* (2022), was featured on Tor.com's Can't Miss Indie Press Speculative Fiction list, and was translated into Italian for Ringworld Sci-Fi in 2023. He founded and edited *BONED*, a literary magazine, and also created two webcomics. Nate is also a husband and a dog dad.

Shaunn Grulkowski has been compared to Warren Ellis and Phillip K. Dick and was once described as what a baby conceived by Kurt Vonnegut and Margaret Atwood would turn out to be. He's at least the fifth best Slavic-Latino-American sci-fi writer in the Baltimore metro area. He's the author *Retcontinuum*, and the editor of *A Stalled Ox* and *The Goldfish* for 1888/Black Hill Press.